*Ki was so certain of his target
that he did not wait...*

Dropping to the ground when he reached the spot he'd chosen, Ki launched his second *shuriken*. It was as effective as the first, though he'd picked a more exacting target. He had to spin the blade in low, almost from ground level, at an angle that brought it sailing upward between the rifleman's shoulder and his hat-brim.

One point of the whirling star dug into the vulnerable triangle between cheekbone and skull and sliced into the raider's brain. His body jerked into a backward bow, and his rifle fell from his nerveless hands as he collapsed. The man was dead before he hit the ground...

•→ WESLEY ELLIS ◆—

LONE STAR

AND THE
RIO GRANDE BANDITS

J (R)

A JOVE BOOK

LONE STAR AND THE RIO GRANDE BANDITS

A Jove Book/published by arrangement with
the author

PRINTING HISTORY
Jove edition/June 1985

ISBN: 0-515-08255-4

Jove books are published by The Berkley Publishing Group,
200 Madison Avenue, New York, N.Y. 10016. The words
"A JOVE BOOK" and the "J" with sunburst are trademarks
belonging to Jove Publications, Inc.

PRINTED IN THE UNITED STATES OF AMERICA

Chapter 1

Jessie woke with a start and sat bolt upright in bed when the loud knocking sounded on the front door of the Circle Star's main house. Both windows in her corner bedroom were open, and the fitful night breeze wafted like a soft caress across her bare shoulders and budded the pink tips of her full breasts.

Once again, the thud of a fist on the downstairs door echoed through the night-silent house. Jessie struck a match from the box that always lay on her bedside table and touched it to the wick of the table lamp. Swinging her feet to the floor, she picked up the dressing gown that lay on the chair beside the table, slipped it on, and hurried from her upstairs bedroom.

Ki was emerging from his own room as Jessie went out her bedroom door, leaving it ajar to shed a glow of faint light in the hall. She said to Ki, "That can't be Ed knocking. He's out riding line with the hands. Besides, if it was Ed, he'd just open the door and call to us."

"It must be one of the men," Ki said as they headed

1

down the stairs. He'd slipped on a pair of the loose-fitting cotton trousers he habitually wore, but had not taken time to step into his sandals. He went on, "And I'd say it's something important, at this time of night. But we'll find out soon enough."

Jessie stopped to light the big lamp in the entrance hall while Ki went on to the door and opened it. Cappy, one of the hands who'd been with the line riders, blinked his eyes and closed them in the sudden flood of lamplight. Then he opened them and looked at Jessie and Ki standing in the doorway.

"I got some real bad news, Miss Jessie," he said, shaking his head soberly. "Brad Close has been shot."

"Is there some kind of trouble on the Box B?" Jessie asked.

"Not as anybody knows yet," Cappy replied. "Me and Skeeter found Brad about an hour after sundown, when we was riding that last stretch of fence over to the northwest of our range. He was laying there by the bobwire just like he was dead. When we got close enough to him we seen the blood, and then we found out he had two bullet holes in him."

Her voice sober, Jessie asked, "Is Brad dead, then?"

"No, ma'am. Leastways, he was still hanging on when I left to come tell you about the shooting."

"Maybe you'd better start from the first and tell us what happened," Ki suggested.

"There ain't an awful lot to tell, Ki," the ranch hand said with a frown. "Me and Skeeter both thought we'd heard some shooting while we was riding along the line fence, but it was so far off we couldn't be right sure. Then, after we seen Brad laying there, we knowed we'd been right. Brad was still holding his pistol, and we found two fired shells in it when we looked at it. That was enough for us to figure out that Brad had got off a couple of shots at whoever it was cut him down. We didn't do no looking around, a'course. We was too busy trying to help him."

"I can understand that," Jessie said, nodding. "And it was too dark by then for you to see much, I'm sure."

"That's right, Miss Jessie," Cappy replied. "It was about an hour after sunset, and we figured we'd better hurry and get Brad home where he could be took care of better."

"You probably wouldn't have found much, anyhow," Ki said. "I imagine that whoever did the shooting didn't stop to see whether Brad was dead or just wounded after he dropped off of his horse."

"Well, anyways," Cappy continued, "soon as me and Skeeter made certain Brad was still alive, I stayed with him and sorta stanched his wounds while Skeeter cut a shuck to get Ed. And Ed said the best thing we could do was take Brad to his own home place, so that's what we done."

"But after you got Brad home, did he recover enough to tell you what had happened?" Jessie asked.

"No, ma'am, Miss Jessie," Cappy replied. "He didn't say nothing for quite a while, even after he come to. There was some lady at the Box B, somebody that's related to Brad. She's sorta taken charge."

"That'd be Brad's niece from the East," Jessie said. "He told me some time ago that he planned to invite her to the Box B for a visit."

"Well, I never did get straight who she was," the ranch hand said. "But when Brad first seen Ed bending over him, he called your name. That's when Ed sent me back here after you and Ki. He figured Brad wanted to tell you something important."

"We'll start for the Box B right away," Jessie said to Ki. She turned back to the ranch hand. "Cappy, will you saddle Sun for me? And a horse for Ki?"

3

"That little pinto I like, Cappy," Ki put in.

"Sure. I know the one. I'll get at it right away."

"When you've got the horses saddled, you'd better go on to the bunkhouse and get some sleep, Cappy," Jessie said. "You've been working all day and half the night. You'll need some rest."

"I'll be glad enough to ride back with you and Ki if you want me to, Miss Jessie," Cappy offered.

"No. That's not necessary. If you men have kept to the schedule Ed told me about, you're due to come in today anyhow."

"Well, we'd rode all but about six miles of the fence along the back range when me and Skeeter found Brad," Cappy said. "Whatever you say, Miss Jessie."

"Just saddle our horses, and then you can call it a day," she told him.

"They'll be out at the hitch rail in front of the house by the time you're ready," Cappy promised. He left, and Jessie and Ki started back upstairs.

"What's your guess, Jessie?" Ki asked. "Rustlers?"

"Either that, or some outlaw heading for the Mexican border, cutting across the Box B and Circle Star range to avoid the roads," Jessie replied. "As far as I know, Brad Close hasn't an enemy in the world. If he has, he's never mentioned one to me in all the years we've been neighbors."

"Brad's been a good neighbor," Ki said thoughtfully. "But rustlers aren't usually active at this time of year, so I suppose you're right about it being somebody running from the law. Plenty of men in that situation will kill anybody who sees them, just to make sure their tracks are covered."

Jessie and Ki were accustomed to moving quickly in emergencies. It took Jessie only a few moments to slip into her ranch clothes—a soft chambray blouse, tight-fitting

4

jeans, and high-heeled boots made to her special order by
Luchesse in San Antonio—and to strap on the belt with her
holstered Colt.

Ki was coming out of his room when she returned to the
hallway. He wore his usual black rope-soled sandals now,
and was just pulling on his leather vest. They went downstairs in silence and out the front door. True to his promise,
Cappy had brought their horses to the hitch rail.

Jessie swung onto Sun's back, the magnificent palomino
stallion whickering excitedly at the prospect of a run. Ki
vaulted into the pinto's saddle, and the two started through
the darkness of the waning night on the familiar trail that
led to the Box B. They rode in the silence of good comrades
who had made many sudden journeys together.

By the time they reached the fence that marked the boundary line between the Circle Star and the Box B, dawn was
beginning to brighten the eastern sky. Ki toed the paint ahead
and opened the gate, waited while Jessie passed through,
then closed the gate behind them. They started along the
Box B trail, but they had gone only a short distance when
Ki reined in.

"What's wrong, Ki?" Jessie asked, pulling on Sun's reins.

"Nothing's wrong," Ki replied. "I've just been thinking
about what Cappy told us. The place where he found Brad
Close can't be much more than a mile from here, and he
and Ed were too busy taking care of Brad to do any looking
around, even if they'd had daylight to search by."

"Meaning you'd like to do some scouting?" she asked.

"If you don't mind riding the rest of the way to the Box
B by yourself."

"I don't mind a bit. I should've thought about trying to
backtrack whoever it was shot Brad."

"There's not much I can do to help at the Box B," Ki

5

went on. "Ed's there, and our men who were riding line, and all the Box B hands, too. And whoever Brad's visitor is."

"You're right." Jessie nodded. "And it won't bother me a bit to go on alone. Do your scouting, Ki. You might find something that'd help us run down whoever ambushed Brad."

Ki reined the pinto around and headed back toward the Circle Star's line fence, one of the few fences on the immense spread. The ranch had been put together by Jessie's father, Alex Starbuck. It was here, on the seemingly endless rolling prairie that stretched below the generally unclouded skies of Southwest Texas, that Alex had found peace and relaxation from the problems of supervising the vast industrial empire he'd created.

Jessie had come to love the Circle Star just as her father did, and after his cowardly assassination by gunmen of the sinister European cartel that was trying to gain control of America's key industries, she'd made the ranch her headquarters, too. She had inherited Alex's battle along with the Starbuck properties, and the ranch was the one place where she could find peace and tranquility. Riding across the prairie on Sun, she would let the warm wind brush past her face to drain away the problems of coping with the ocean shipping lines, railroads and mines, banks and mills that constituted the Starbuck holdings.

Ki turned once to look back at Jessie, erect in the saddle of the big palomino stallion, her small figure silhouetted against the slowly brightening sky. Then he reached the line fence, and he toed the pinto pony to move parallel to the barbwire strands as he searched for the place where Brad Close had fallen to the bullets of a would-be assassin.

He found the spot with surprisingly little trouble, a patch of ground on both sides of the fence where horses had been reined in and tethered. Though the soil in that area of arid

6

Southwest Texas was rock hard almost everywhere, the constant movement of several tethered horses always left the thin grass broken and scuffed for several days.

Ki was certain he'd found the place he was looking for when he saw an ugly brownish red stain in the tan soil where the grass had been trampled by the hooves of restless horses. He dismounted and led his horse up to the spot. After he'd looked at the place for a moment, he began moving slowly along the tightly stretched barbwire, surveying the ground carefully as he advanced.

Less than fifty yards from the spot where Close had fallen, Ki's sharp eyes caught the glint of brass on the earth. He dropped the reins to let the pinto pony stand, walked up to the shining shell cases, and hunkered down.

A glance was all that Ki needed to identify the shells as having been fired from a .30-.30 Winchester. The ejector marks on their bases were plainly visible in the constantly brightening light. The spent cartridges had been ejected within inches of one another, a sign that the man who'd fired them had stood in one spot while he shot.

A careful survey did not reveal any hoofprints on the ground around the spent casings, which told Ki that whoever fired the rifle had left his horse some distance away and walked to the fence, probably after he'd seen Close riding up in the distance. Rising to his feet, Ki again scanned the barren terrain in all directions. The land here was generally level, though humps here and there indicated that it was dotted with small depressions in which a riderless horse might have been left to stand without being readily noticed.

Moving slowly, his eyes fixed on the ground, Ki began searching the area on the Box B side of the line fence. He moved in a series of half circles that were designed to cover the greatest amount of ground in the shortest possible time. After covering an area of perhaps a hundred yards from his pony without discovering any signs of the intruder, Ki stopped, perplexed, and took a second look at the surrounding terrain.

From his examination of the spot where Brad Close had fallen, Ki was convinced that whoever had fired the shots must have been riding from the northeast when he encountered the fence. Ki was still looking at the wide expanse of ground that stretched from the line fence toward the steadily brightening horizon, seeking further evidence of the assailant's approach, when he glimpsed the suggestion of a movement in the middle distance. The suggestion was all that Ki needed. In less than an eye wink he dropped flat and began rolling away from the line fence.

Ki's swift reflexes, honed by experience to a razor's edge, saved him this time as they had done so often in the past. He'd barely flattened himself on the ground when the form of a man shouldering a rifle popped up from a small depression to his right. The rifle barked, and a slug kicked up dust beyond the fence in line with the spot where Ki had been standing. Before the echoes of the rifle shot had died away and the morning air was quiet again, the rifleman had vanished.

For several moments Ki stayed motionless, seeking the best angle to approach the little hollow in which his attacker was hiding. The bare earth offered no cover. The land between him and the little hump that marked the depression was billiard-table flat. Not even a clump of weeds grew between him and his unknown assailant. There was nothing at all to mask his movement in approaching the concealed sniper.

Like a jack-in-the-box, the rifleman popped up and fired again. Ki got no more than a glimpse of a swarthy, bearded face in the few seconds that passed before the sniper had loosed his second shot and vanished. By this time, though,

Ki was half-crawling, half-rolling in *budo* style toward the small hollow where the would-be assassin was hiding.

Arduous training by his master instructor in warrior tactics enabled Ki to belly-crawl and roll forward while flat on the ground with almost as much speed as if he'd been on his feet and running. As he started across the forty or fifty yards that stretched between him and the depression, Ki took a *shuriken* from one of the many pockets in his leather vest. He held the little circular throwing blade ready in his hand, positive that the man in the depression was not going to risk letting him get closer.

When the sniper showed himself again, Ki was prepared. The instant the rifleman's head showed above the rim of the hollow, Ki launched the *shuriken* with a skill and speed born of long, patient practice. His movements were so swift that the man who'd shot at him was still lowering his head to the stock to aim when the wicked blade, its star-shaped points honed razor keen, spun through the air in a low arc that ended unerringly in the few exposed inches of the rifleman's throat, a fraction of an inch above the stock of the weapon.

Even after the *shuriken*'s blade had buried itself in his throat, the attacker triggered his shot with his dying reflex. By this time, though, the rifle's muzzle was already beginning to slant upward, and the slug whistled past Ki well above his head. Ki lay motionless for a few seconds, watching the man's gun fall unheeded from his listless hands as he crumpled slowly to the ground, his wound draining his life away.

Although the mysterious shootist had dropped out of sight in the hollow where he'd been holed up, Ki knew his assailant was dead. He got to his feet and walked to the hollow. Looking down into the little depression, he understood why the mystery man had not left the scene. The body of the rifleman had dropped to earth at the side of a dead horse.

A pool of dark blood that had poured from the horse's wound covered a patch of earth in the hollow's bottom; the blood was still blackening and was not yet totally congealed. The dead horse and the patch of bloody earth beside it told Ki the story as clearly as if he'd witnessed the attempt the stranger had made on Brad Close's life.

Remembering that Cappy had mentioned finding two discharged shells in the Box B owner's Colt, Ki realized that one of the shots Close had fired struck the mystery man's horse. Without a mount, probably uncertain of himself in the darkness and on strange terrain, the attacker had elected to wait until daylight to move on. In the beginning dawn, he'd seen Ki approaching and had holed up in the hollow beside his dead mount, planning to shoot Ki, take the pinto, and escape. Only Ki's quick reactions and instant counterattack had foiled his scheme.

There still remained the mystery of the dead man's identity and his reason for attempting to kill the owner of the Box B. Ki knew the small handful of ranchers whose land touched the Circle Star range, and of the group, he'd always considered Brad Close to be the kindest and most easy-going.

Well past the prime of life, Close felt no need to expand his holdings the way some of the later arrivals did. He kept a light hand on the reins in his management of the spread, got along well with his neighbors and his own men, and was quick to offer help in times of trouble—though he'd seldom been forced to ask others to help him.

One of Alex Starbuck's best friends, Close had stood by Jessie's side during the trying period after Alex's cruel murder, and though no one could ever replace Alex in her heart, Jessie had come to look on him as a sort of foster father, standing beside her in place of the real father she'd lost. Ki could not think of any reason other than the hand of blind fate that would have made Close the target of a killer's bullet.

A pair of saddlebags lay a short distance from the carcass of the horse. Ki stepped over and picked them up, looking for a clue to the identity of the dead man. The bags contained only a stack of tortillas wrapped in a tattered bandanna, and a grease-stained grocer's bag holding a lump of cheese. Obviously, the stranger had been moving fast and traveling light, and Ki's suspicions deepened.

His face soberly thoughtful, Ki moved to the side of the dead rifleman. For a moment he studied the features of the motionless figure sprawled on the hard earth near the dead horse. Frozen in the stillness of death, there was nothing unusual about him, nothing that would have set him apart in a room full of cowhands. The rifleman had needed a shave, but most of the men on the area's isolated spreads didn't shave oftener than once a week. There were no scars, no special features that would have drawn the notice of a casual observer.

Dropping to one knee, Ki began exploring the dead man's pockets. His vest pockets yielded a sack of Bull Durham tobacco, a folder of cigarette papers, and a scant handful of matches. In one pocket of his jeans Ki found a small number of coins, a total of less than ten dollars. Another pocket yielded a jackknife, and a hip pocket contained a wrinkled bandanna.

That was all. There was no article of any sort that would have given a clue to the dead man's name, where he'd come from, or where he'd been going. Ki was frowning when he finished his search. Few men, even on the boundless and impersonal prairies, traveled without some hint of their past or present.

Ki's eyes fell on the dead man's gunbelt, and he drew

the revolver nestled in it. The gun was a single-action .44-40 Remington, almost an exact copy of the much more popular Colt. Hefting the heavy weapon for a moment, Ki thumbed the hammer to half cock and opened the loading port to see whether the gun had been fired. As he revolved the cylinder he saw that the shells were all unfired. The six chambers held only five cartridges—not unusual, since it was a standard precaution to carry a six-shot revolver with the hammer resting on an empty chamber.

Then, just as he raised his hand to close the loading port, Ki saw a rolled slip of paper nestled in the chamber that held no shell. For a moment the paper defied his efforts to remove it, but at last he blew hard into the loading port and managed to get hold of it. He drew it out carefully and spread it flat on his knee.

Only four lines of writing were on the narrow slip: "Brad Close. Box B ranch next to Circle Star. Do it right away. Pay is $1000.00."

Chapter 2

Dawnlight's soft, pearly gray glow had taken over the rim of the horizon when Jessie arrived at the Box B Ranch, but the pink tinge of sunrise had not yet colored the sky. Yellowish lamplight glowed from the windows of both the main house and bunkhouse, and there were saddled horses standing at the hitch rails in front of each of them. Enough ranch hands to make a roundup crew, some from the Box B, some from the Circle Star, were sitting on the bunkhouse steps or hunkered down on the hardpacked soil in front of it.

Skeeter, the Circle Star hand who'd been with Cappy, came over to take Jessie's horse as she swung out of the saddle.

"How's Brad doing?" Jessie asked, handing him Sun's reins.

"Last word we got from the house was that he's holding up pretty good," Skeeter replied. "That was a while ago, but I don't guess things've changed much."

Jessie nodded and went into the main house. Brad Close had not built the Box B to the high standards Alex Starbuck had insisted on at the Circle Star. The living room was small and furnished strictly for utility. A tall potbellied stove stood in one corner and there were two easy chairs, several smaller chairs and a sofa, a pair of lamp tables, and a gun rack. The floor was covered with a utilitarian Wilton carpet of a subdued pattern.

Ed Wright, the Circle Star foreman, was sitting in front of the stove with a cup of coffee in his hand. He stood up when he saw Jessie, and said, "I figured you oughta be getting here about now, Jessie. Last word I had from Brad's bedroom, he was a little bit better."

"That's good news," Jessie said. "But you saw him right after the boys found him, Ed. Do you think he'll pull through?"

"Hard to tell." Wright frowned. "I wouldn't have given him much of a chance when we found him. He took one slug low on his left side and another one just over his belly. And he'd bled a terrible lot. By the time we got him bandaged up enough to move him here, he was in pretty bad shape. But he was still alive when we got him here, so maybe he'll make it."

"Who's looking after him?"

"His niece from back east. Her name's Linda something. I got introduced, but things was pretty roiled up right then. And Hardrock's in there with her."

Hardrock was the Box B cook. On most of the ranches in such isolated areas as the vast, empty plains of the Southwest, cooks did double duty: when necessary, they also served as doctors.

"I don't suppose he's been able to do much talking yet, though," Jessie said.

"If he's said anything, nobody's passed the word to me," Wright told her. "When I got to where Cappy and Skeeter

14

found him, all Brad was able to say was your name."

"He asked for me?"

"He said 'Jessie' three or four times," the foreman said with a nod. "He went under again when we started to move him; then after we got him here, he came to just long enough to know he was home. That's when he called your name again. I figured it was important enough to send Cappy back to tell you."

"You did exactly right, Ed," Jessie assured the foreman. "If Brad wants me here, he's got a good reason."

"I was just waiting for you and Ki to get here before I took our boys back to work," Wright went on. "There's nothing they can do here to help."

"Of course, Ed." Jessie nodded. "Ki will be here pretty soon, and we'll stay as long as we're needed."

"Was there something wrong at the Circle Star that kept Ki from coming with you?"

"No, of course not. We left together, but he stopped to take a look at the place where Brad got shot. He thought he might pick up the trail of whoever did the shooting."

Wright nodded and said, "We'll get on back to the Circle Star, then. But maybe I'd better call Brad's niece and introduce you to her before we start."

"Yes, that'd be a good idea," Jessie agreed.

She followed Wright to the bedroom door. He tapped softly, and a woman called, "Yes? Come in."

Wright opened the door a crack and lowered his voice to say, "Miss Starbuck's here, if Brad's awake and still wants to talk to her."

There was a stirring in the bedroom, and a young woman opened the door and slipped through to join Jessie and Wright. Jessie placed her age as being in the early or middle twenties. Her dark blond hair was caught up in a bun on

15

the back of her head, and she had pale blue eyes set in a rounded face with a slightly snubbed nose. There was nothing extraordinary about either her face or figure; she was the sort of person who would not draw a second glance if encountered in a crowd. She was wearing a plain gingham housedress, belted at the waist.

The young woman did not extend her hand, but looked at Jessie for a moment. Then she said, "I'm Linda Jackson, Miss Starbuck."

"Yes, Brad's niece." Jessie nodded. "I've heard him speak of you. I'm pleased to meet you, Miss Jackson, but I wish it could've been under more fortunate circumstances."

"I know," Linda agreed. "But it looks like Uncle Brad's going to be all right. He's dozing now, and I hope he'll stay asleep. That's why I came out here instead of inviting you in."

"Of course," Jessie replied. "I understand. And you're sure Brad's all right?"

"Well, that's what Hardrock says, and he knows a lot more than I do about things like bullet wounds." Linda motioned to the divan. "Please sit down, Miss Starbuck."

"Jessie, if you don't mind," Jessie said. "Out here, we're not very formal. But I'm sure you've discovered that by now."

"I have, but I still can't get used to it," Linda told her as they sat down on the divan. "I never have seen a man who was shot before. I'll tell you, it scared me pretty bad."

"Yes." Jessie nodded. "Violence does scare folks who aren't used to it."

Linda sat silently for a moment, studying Jessie covertly. At last she said, "I guess you know more about Uncle Brad than I do, Jessie. Do you know why anybody'd want to shoot him?"

16

Jessie shook her head. "I'd have sworn that Brad doesn't have an enemy in the world. He's one of the nicest, gentlest men I've ever known."

"But somebody hated him enough to shoot him."

"I have a hunch that whoever it was didn't even know your uncle, Linda," Jessie said. "I think Brad just accidentally ran into an outlaw who was trying to get down south of the border, into Mexico."

"That's what Hardrock thinks too. My goodness, Jessie! Do you have outlaws around here all the time?"

"Of course not! The West's not at all wild, the way you folks who live in the East think it is."

"Well, I don't know. From what I've seen of it, though, I don't like it."

"I'm sure you'd change your mind if you lived here, Linda. This part of the country's—" Jessie stopped short as the door to the bedroom opened and Hardrock stuck his head out.

"Brad's wide-awake again, Miss Linda," the cook said. "He keeps asking when Miss Jessie's gonna git here. I ain't told him yet that you was here, Miss Jessie. Me and Miss Linda was wondering if talking to you'd upset him or soothe him down."

"Knowing Brad, he's not going to rest until he rids his mind of whatever it is he wants to tell me," Jessie replied. She looked from Hardrock to Linda, then went on, "I really think I'd better go in and talk to him. Maybe then he'll settle down and go to sleep."

"I guess maybe you're right," Hardrock agreed.

Linda hesitated for a moment, then said, "Yes, it might help if Uncle Brad talks to you, Jessie. Go on in. I'll wait out here."

Moving quietly, Jessie went into the bedroom. The window shades were drawn, and a lamp in one corner had been turned low, casting the dimmest possible light in the room. Hardrock entered the room behind Jessie and walked with her to the bed. He nodded to her and put his forefinger across his lips.

Brad Close lay on the bed, his eyes closed. His gray moustache looked unnaturally dark against his face, which was almost as white as the sheet that covered him to the waist. Above the sheet, bloodstained bandages were wrapped around the wounds in his chest and stomach. The bandages rose and fell gently as he breathed.

Jessie said in a barely audible whisper, "If he's asleep, I'll just slip back into the living room. You can tell me when he wakes up."

Before Hardrock could reply, Brad opened his eyes and tried to focus them on Jessie, but he did not seem able to. His voice a hoarse, rasping whisper, he asked, "Is that you, Jessie?"

"Yes, Brad. I got here as soon as I could when I heard what happened to you."

"Oh, I knew you wouldn't waste no time after you got word I'd been shot," Brad said. "But don't worry, I'm gonna be your neighbor for a good while yet."

"I'm glad," Jessie told him. "But you need rest now more than you need to talk to me. Why don't you sleep awhile, and we can have our talk after you wake up."

"I'd like it better if we talked now," the Box B owner replied. "Hardrock, you better go tend to getting the boys fed breakfast or supper or whatever meal they got coming. I don't know what time it is, but I know you been here by me since Jessie's men brought me home."

"It's still before breakfast, Brad," the cook said. "But I reckon you wanta talk private to Miss Jessie, so I'll go take care of the hands." He stood up and said to Jessie, "You just call if you need me, and I'll come a-running."

"Don't worry, I will," Jessie promised. She waited until the cook left the room, then sat down in the chair beside Brad's bed. She told the wounded rancher, "Please don't feel like you have to talk to me right now, Brad. You don't have to be in a hurry to tell me what's on your mind. I'm going to stay here with you until you're better."

"Now, that's a right neighborly thing to do, Jessie, but don't feel like you got to stay here lessen you just want to. I got Hardrock and the boys to look after me."

"And your niece, too," Jessie put in.

"Oh, her," Brad said.

Despite the weakness of his voice, Jessie could read the distaste that he put into the two words. She frowned as she said, "You sound like you've had a falling-out with her."

"Never had anything to fall out of, Jessie," Brad rasped. "This is the third time I've seen Linda since she was knee-high to a puddle duck."

"And she didn't grow up to be what you expected?"

"Not so's you'd notice."

"She's not your daughter, Brad. Just your niece. Maybe you expect too much of her."

"Maybe. But she's the only kith and kin I got, aside from her mother. And Nellie—that's her mother—we ain't blood kin. She's my brother's widow, and I ain't been around her since I left home to go off to the War. The last time I seen her was ten years ago, when my brother died and left her a widow, and I took the train back east to his funeral."

Brad had raised his head while he was talking, and now he let it fall back on the pillow and closed his eyes. Jessie saw that his long speech had exhausted him, and she sat quietly, hoping he'd drop off to sleep. After he lay mo-

19

tionless for several minutes, though, Close opened his eyes again and looked up at her.

"I sorta talked myself out, didn't I, Jessie?" he said with a wry smile.

"You shouldn't be talking at all," Jessie told him. "Just lie quiet, Brad, and try to go to sleep."

"That's what Linda and Hardrock been telling me ever since I got here," Close replied. "And maybe I can sleep after I get what I got to tell you off of my mind."

"Go ahead, Brad," she urged. "Tell me so you can rest."

"That fellow who plugged me, Jessie. I got more'n a hunch he wasn't just some outlaw on the run, the way Ed and Hardrock figure. He was laying for me and nobody else."

Jessie's eyes widened as she asked, "Why, Brad? You're not the kind of man who makes enemies. At least not enemies who want to kill you."

"Oh, I rub folks the wrong way now and again," Close said. "But this time I figure I rubbed the wrong man backwards."

"Who? Who's the wrong man, Brad?"

"I was aiming to tell you this, but you was gone on one of your trips when it happened, and I ain't had a chance since," Close said.

Almost before he'd finished speaking, his eyelids fluttered closed and his head fell back on the pillow. Worried, Jessie felt his wrist, but his pulse was steady though weak. She felt his forehead, which was cool, and his breathing was as regular as his pulse. She sat quietly then, waiting for his strength to return. After a short while he opened his eyes again.

"I ain't all that bad off, Jessie," he said. "I hurt and I lost a lot of blood, I guess, which is what's got me so tired

20

and weak. But I been in worse shape before and got up and went about my business, and I aim to do it again."

"Of course you will, Brad," she assured him. "But don't you think you ought to do your resting now and talk later?"

"Later might be too late," he replied stubbornly. "Now you just set there and listen, and when I get tired of talking, I'll close my eyes and rest."

"All right," she agreed. "Just don't overdo."

"I figure that fellow that's been trying to buy me out is the one who's back of this shooting," Close began. Jessie's eyes widened, but she kept her promise and said nothing.

"It started five or six months ago," Close went on. "Some fellow I never seen before—called hisself Morgan—showed up one day and said he was out buying cattle range for some kind of beef-selling syndicate that'd just been put together back east. Wanted to know what I'd take for the Box B, and when I told him I wasn't interested in selling out, he begun making offers."

Again Close fell silent, and Jessie sat quietly, noting no change in his condition. After the old rancher had lain still for several minutes, breathing deeply, he opened his eyes and resumed his story.

"Well, to cut it short, this fellow Morgan rode off mad. Then a week or so later, he come back with another offer. It was a lot more'n I figure this place to be worth, but my dander was up, so I just kept on saying no till he stomped off again."

"And he hasn't been back?"

"Not as I know. But the boys tell me they seen hoof tracks in places they ain't been riding, so I figure somebody's been keeping tabs on the place."

"Spying on you, Brad?"

"I guess you'd call it that."

"Did the man who called himself Morgan mention any names of the others in the syndicate?"

Close shook his head weakly and said, "He called it the American National Meat Company, but he didn't call no names. Now, you keep quiet like you said you would and let me go on."

"I'm sorry," Jessie apologized. "I won't interrupt again."

After he'd rested once more, Close went on. "Now, I never have told you nor nobody else this, Jessie, because I promised your daddy I wouldn't. But about a year before he was gunned down, Alex come to me and said he'd consider it a favor if I'd give him first refusal should I ever decide to sell the Box B. I told him I aimed to leave it to my kin, and he said he wasn't going to push me about deciding nothing, but if I changed my mind, to let him know."

Again Brad Close fell silent. Jessie waited until she was sure he wasn't going to continue, then said, "Don't try to answer me until you're ready to, but have you changed your mind?"

Close did not reply at once, but lay still, his eyes shut, his chest rising and falling as he breathed deeply. For a moment Jessie thought he'd dropped off to sleep again, and she remained silent. At last he opened his eyes and started talking again.

"You know, Jessie, I never did talk much with your daddy about his business," he said. "Oh, I knew he had a lot of irons in the fire, and even before he was killed I knew he had some pretty mean enemies that was working against him. And though I ain't mentioned it to you, I guessed you took up right where he left off. You don't need to say nothing, but I'd like to know if I'm right."

"You're right, Brad," Jessie answered quickly. "I intend

22

to carry on what Alex was doing. But that's all I want to say about it. Might be dangerous for you to know too much."

"I figured something out, Jessie. That feller who come trying to buy the Box B wasn't no friend of yours, and I sorta guessed he didn't aim to do you no good was I to've sold him the ranch."

"Is that why you refused?"

Brad shook his head. "No. I aimed to leave the place to the only kin I got—Linda and her mother."

"That's what you ought to do, then."

"You didn't understand me, Jessie. I said I aimed to do that until just the other day. Now, I ain't so sure."

"You've changed your mind?"

"Linda's changed my mind for me. I told her I wanted to put her and her mother in my will to inherit the Box B, and she said they didn't want no part of it."

Jessie spoke quickly. "If it'd help any, you can tell them that if you left them the Box B and they didn't want it, I'd be glad to buy it from them at a fair price."

"They just plain don't want it," Close said. His weakness did not keep anger from creeping into his voice. "They belong to one of them funny religions that teaches 'em having money's bad for folks. And besides that, Linda said they don't wanta feel beholden to me for anything."

"You don't think they'd change their minds?"

"I was sorta hoping you might try talking to Linda. Get her off by herself and see if you can make her act reasonable. That's why I was heading for the Circle Star when I got shot, to ask you if you'd try."

"Well, I'll be glad to talk to her, Brad," Jessie said slowly. "But if they're refusing your offer because of some religious belief, I'm not sure it'd do any good."

"You got a nice way of putting things. Maybe you could

23

talk some sense into her head," Close told her. "It won't hurt none to try, will it?"

"I'll do the best I can," Jessie promised.

"Sure. I know you will, Jessie. You better get started right now, though. Linda's dead set on leaving. Wants to start back home tomorrow. She didn't tell me that until yesterday, which is why I didn't ride over to ask you sooner. I'd take it as a special favor if you talk to her right now. Hardrock can set with me while you're with Linda."

When Hardrock had replaced Jessie in the chair beside Brad's bed, Jessie spoke to Linda in the living room. "You've been under a strain, being kept close to your uncle's bed such a long time. Wouldn't you like to stroll around for a few minutes with me outside? It'd give us a chance to chat and get acquainted, and I think we could both use a breath of fresh air."

"I suppose," Linda answered with a shrug.

Jessie led the way outside. The area around the house was clear now, with the Box B men back at their jobs and the Circle Star hands on their way home. The sun was well above the horizon by now, but the air was still cool.

"I think this is the time of day when I like this country best," Jessie said as they walked slowly between the house and the bunkhouse to stand in the sunshine. "Everything fresh and clean at the start of a new day."

Linda looked at the prairie, stretching in all directions to a seemingly endless horizon. She said, "I guess it's all right, but it's so—well, so empty. It—maybe it sort of scares me."

"Is that why you don't want to take your uncle's offer to leave the Box B to you and your mother?"

"Did Uncle Brad tell you that?"

"Yes. Neighbors don't have many secrets from one another in this part of the country, Linda."

24

"Well, I don't want to hear any of yours, and I don't want to talk about Uncle Brad willing us the ranch."

Linda turned and started back toward the house. Jessie followed her. They were turning the corner to the front of the house just as Ki rode up. The body of the man he'd killed lay draped in front of him, and the corpse's arms and head and legs were swaying in rhythm with the movement of his pony.

Linda saw the body and screamed. "We're all going to be killed!" she cried. Still screaming, she ran into the house and slammed the door.

Chapter 3

"Linda!" Jessie called. She realized at once that she'd spoken too late; the fleeing girl was already in the house and was closing the door. Turning to Ki, she said, "I'm curious about what you found, but before you tell me what happened, I've got to go in and keep Linda from disturbing Brad. While I'm gone, you'd better go behind the bunkhouse and unload that body."

"Maybe I shouldn't have brought the body back here," Ki said. "But he's the man who shot Brad, and I wanted to ask the Box B hands if any of them had seen him around the place earlier."

"It's not your fault, Ki," Jessie replied. "But we'll talk later, after I've gotten Linda calmed down."

Ki toed the pinto around the bunkhouse, and Jessie hurried into the house. The bedroom door stood open, and she could hear the voices of Linda and Hardrock mingling in a confused jumble. She went to the door. Brad Close was lying propped up on the bed, obviously upset by the commotion, while Hardrock and Linda stood between the bed

26

and the door, shouting at one another.

"Stop it, you two!" Jessie commanded sharply. Both Linda and Hardrock turned to look at her, their loud voices suddenly silent. Jessie went on, "Hardrock, do what you can to get Brad calmed down. Linda, you come with me!"

Too surprised to argue, Linda followed Jessie from the room. Hardrock was already talking to Brad in soothing tones, and before Jessie pulled the door closed a quick glance assured her that the old rancher had relaxed a bit already.

"Let's go outside," Jessie suggested. "Ki's put the body where you won't have to look at it."

"I—I guess I acted silly, didn't I?" Linda said hesitatingly. "But I never saw anything like that dead man until now. All the corpses I've seen were in coffins, laid out nice and peaceful. This one was all bloody and..." Her voice faded and trailed off.

"Death's not pretty or peaceful a lot of the time," Jessie reminded the girl. "But I know that in the East you don't often see the kind of things we do here in the West from time to time."

"I was more scared of that awful Chinese man than I was of the body," Linda protested. "For all I knew, he was ready to kill all of us!"

"That awful man, as you call him, isn't awful at all, and you'll find that out very soon," Jessie said severely as she led Linda to the door. "His name is Ki, and he's not Chinese, but half Japanese and half American. He's also my very trusted helper and friend, just as he was my father's."

Ki had returned from dropping off the corpse and was wrapping the pinto's reins around the bunkhouse hitch rail when Jessie and Linda got outside. He looked questioningly at Jessie as she led Linda toward him.

"It's all right," Jessie said quickly. "This is Brad Close's niece, Linda. She got frightened and panicked, but she's all right now. Linda, this is Ki."

"Linda," Ki said, bobbing his head and shoulders in a small half bow. "I didn't mean to startle you, but the body I brought in is that of the man who shot your uncle. I wanted to find out if any of the ranch hands had seen him lurking around here before the shooting."

Looking at Ki with barely concealed curiosity, she asked, "Did you kill him?"

"Yes. But we won't talk about that now," Ki replied. "If it will make you feel any better, he started shooting at me, and I had to kill him to save my own life."

"I'm sorry I got all excited the way I did," Linda said. "But like I told Jessie, I never saw a thing like that before."

"And I hope you won't have to see anything like it again," Ki said soberly. "But there's something important I need to talk about with Jessie. Would you mind if we went off a little way for a few minutes?"

Linda shook her head. "No. But I think I'll go back inside. I feel a lot safer indoors than I do out here."

After Linda left, Jessie asked Ki, "You're sure that man you killed was the one who shot Brad?"

"Positive," Ki answered. "If you remember what Cappy told us, they could tell from Brad's gun that he'd fired two shots. One of them must've hit the killer's horse, and with it dead, he couldn't get away. He was still holed up in a little dry wash when I got there, and started shooting at me. I didn't have any choice but to kill him. I'd much rather have taken him alive so we could've questioned him."

"I see." Jessie nodded. "And there wasn't anything on him that would give us a clue to who he was or why he shot Brad?"

"There certainly was." Ki took out the slip of paper he'd found in the empty chamber of the dead gunman's revolver

28

and handed it to Jessie. "This tells us at least part of the story."

Jessie scanned the few words scribbled on the narrow slip, then looked up at Ki, a thoughtful frown growing on her face. "Instructions to a hired killer," she said. "And I'm sure I know who wrote this—or instructed somebody to write it."

Jessie told Ki of the offer to buy the Box B that the mysterious Morgan had made Brad, how it had been repeated several times, and how Brad had persisted in refusing to sell.

"Does this smell as bad to you as it does to me?" Ki asked.

Jessie nodded. "The cartel, of course. I've been wondering when they'd try to get a fixed position on the edge of the Circle Star, where they'd have a base to attack us from. It seems they finally decided on this spread of Brad's."

"It's you who's their target, Jessie," Ki pointed out. "Not the ranch."

"Certainly, Ki. You and I have known that all along. We've just never put it into words before."

"Is Brad going to get well?" Ki asked. "Because if he is, we certainly won't have to worry about him selling to anybody."

"Brad will be all right," Jessie assured him. "And he's seen through the offer to buy him out, even though he doesn't know anything about the cartel and its plotting. Oh, he suspects a lot, but he doesn't know anything for sure."

"What about Linda?" Ki asked. "Where does she fit in?"

Using as few words as possible, Jessie quickly sketched the family situation that Brad faced, and her promise to try to talk with Linda about it. When she'd finished her explanation, Ki nodded.

"Then you won't have to worry about the cartel getting

a foothold so close to the Circle Star," he said.

"No. I know I can trust Brad to see to that, even if he doesn't know all the ins and outs of the situation. But we'd better go in and see what's happening. Brad's still weak, and I don't want Linda upsetting him."

Linda was sitting quietly on the divan when Jessie and Ki got inside, and the door to Brad's bedroom was closed. Before Jessie or Ki could speak, Linda said, "I guess Uncle Brad's told you I've made up my mind to start back home tomorrow, Jessie. He wants me to stay, but will you help me persuade him it's the right thing for me to do?"

"Of course, if that's what you want," Jessie said. "But what are you going to tell him about the Box B?"

"I told him Mama and I just don't want it."

"Yes, that's what he said. And I told him that if he willed it to you, and you and your mother don't want it, I'll buy it from you."

"But Mama and I are religious people," Linda protested. "We don't believe in—"

"I understand," Jessie assured her. "But think of all the charitable works your church could put that money to. Now, if you accept my offer, I'll write an agreement to sell that you can take back for your mother to sign, and I'll give you my written agreement to buy."

"I'm sure that'll suit Mama just fine," Linda said. "And I know it suits me, so long as the money gets put in the service of the church. I don't know how to thank you for being so nice, Jessie. Now all we've got to do is tell Uncle Brad."

When Linda told Brad her decision and explained the agreement she'd made with Jessie, the old rancher nodded slowly. He said, "It's about what I figured you'd do, Linda. And Jessie must've told you I want her to have the ranch if you and your ma don't take it over and run it."

30

"Yes, Uncle Brad. And I hope you understand why I want to go home right away instead of staying till you get well."

"Sure," he replied. "There's folks that don't like it out here in the West, and you and your mama are two of 'em. Well, you've made a deal that'll satisfy all of us, so I don't see any reason for you to stay any longer in a place you don't like."

"Then I'll pack and get ready to catch the eastbound train in the morning," Linda said. For the first time, her voice sounded happy.

"Wait a minute," Brad said. "That train goes past the whistle-stop real early. You'll have to leave right after supper if you wanta catch it."

Linda's smile turned into a worried frown. "Oh, my! I'd forgotten that. But there's got to be a way for me to catch it!"

"I'm sure there is," Jessie said. "It's only a four-hour ride to the whistle-stop, and Brad's got plenty of horses."

"I can't ride horseback, Jessie," Linda confessed. "I never had a chance to learn. And I've got two big suitcases."

"I picked her up in the spring wagon when she got here," Brad said. "And you're forgetting that it's ten or twelve miles further to the siding from the Box B than it is from the Circle Star. She'll have to leave here pretty soon after supper to be sure of getting there in time to catch that train."

"I'll be glad to drive the wagon," Jessie offered.

Brad shook his head. "I told Hardrock you'd set with me tonight, Jessie," Brad said. "Him and the boys need to catch up on the work they couldn't do when they was looking after me."

"Ki, of course!" Jessie exclaimed. "He can drive the wagon." She turned to Linda. "You wouldn't be afraid to ride with him, would you?"

31

"Goodness, no! I only talked to him a minute or so, but I could see right away he wasn't what I'd thought he was at first."

"It's settled, then," Brad said. "Now you go pack, Linda. The sooner after supper you start, the better."

"My goodness," Linda said. "If anybody'd told me after I saw you with that dead man across the saddle that I'd be sitting next to you on this wagon seat now, I wouldn't have believed them."

"I'm really sorry I upset you, Linda," Ki told her. "I know it must've been a shock."

"Well, that's over and done with," she assured him.

"Of course," Ki agreed. "And I think we're both glad."

"I know I am," she replied. They rode in silence for a few minutes, and then Linda said, "Ki. I never knew anybody who had a name like that. What's the rest of it?"

"There isn't any rest of it," he replied. "Just Ki."

"Don't Japanese people have more than one name?"

"Of course. But I—well, I have good reasons to use only one. Personal reasons," he added quickly.

"I see."

Ki could tell from the tone of Linda's voice that she did not see, but he made no comment.

They rode on in silence through the quiet night. The moon was full, and it bathed the land in a silver light that was kinder to the prairie than the brilliant light of the sun. Instead of revealing the barrenness of the gently rolling terrain, the moonlight concealed its stark harshness, making it look like an undulating carpet of softly textured grasses that invited the feet of the weary traveler.

"This is the first time since I've been here that I've been out this far at night," Linda said. "Everything looks different. It's right pretty, not like it is in the daytime."

"This country's like a beautiful woman, Linda," Ki told her. "It might not look the same today as it did yesterday, but it's always pretty, night or day."

"My goodness! You talk like a poet, Ki!"

"I'm not. But I was brought up to recognize beauty when I see it, whether it's in the countryside or a painting or a piece of fine pottery."

"You see! I knew you were a poet!" When Ki did not reply, Linda sat silent for a few moments, then asked, "Do you think I'm pretty, Ki?"

"Of course you are. Hasn't anybody ever told you that?"

"Just one person. Donnie—he's the boy I ran away with a couple of years ago and was going to marry."

Ki hid his surprise at her words. Though he'd learned that some quality he possessed led women to confide in him, he'd never quite gotten used to accepting their confessions. "But you didn't marry him?" he asked.

Linda shook her head. "No. We decided we'd hide from his folks and my mother for a while, but they found us after about three weeks. Then his folks moved away and took him with them."

"He never did try to find you again?"

"If he did, I didn't know anything about it."

"I'm sorry," Ki said. "You might've been very happy."

"I guess. And I've never found anybody else I could feel about like I felt about him."

"You mean you've tried to love other men?"

"Yes." After a moment's silence, Linda went on, "Don't you see, Ki, I don't have anything to lose. Too many people back home know that Donnie and I lived together three weeks without being married. That makes me a bad woman."

"But you don't feel like you're bad, do you?"

"Certainly not! I enjoyed every minute of those three weeks with Donnie." Again she sat in silence for several

33

minutes while the wagon bumped along. Then she said, "I don't know why I've told you all this, you being almost a stranger. But as long as I've started, I'll tell you the rest. I enjoy being with a man, Ki. I guess I always will, now. And I intend to go on enjoying it just as long as I feel the way I do!"

Ki said quietly, "If it'll make you easier, Linda, you're not the only woman who feels the way you do."

"I've started to learn that," she replied. She paused again, and asked, "How do you feel, Ki? Are you and Jessie—"

"No," Ki answered quickly. "Jessie is my friend. She'll always be my friend, just as her father was."

"Then would you like to stop for a while?" Linda asked. "I guess we've got a little time, and there's nobody going to be watching us out here on this prairie."

"I'd enjoy it," Ki replied. "As long as you're sure—"

"I'm sure," she broke in. "I've been getting itchier by the minute almost since we started. I guess that must be why I told you all about myself. Does that make any difference?"

"No. You've just been honest."

"Then stop the wagon whenever you want to, Ki. I'm ready right now."

Ki reined in the horse and looped the leathers around the seat-rail. He'd barely secured them before Linda began climbing into the wagon bed. By the time Ki stepped over the seat and joined her, she was bending down to grasp the hem of her skirt.

"We don't have to hurry," he said. "There's plenty of time for us to undress."

"You're sure?"

"Yes. I allowed an extra hour or so. Don't worry, Linda. I'll get you on the train."

"Good. I like it better when I'm naked." Linda turned

34

around and said, "Undo my dress buttons, Ki. I could, but it feels nice to have you do it."

As Ki worked the buttons free of their loops, he could feel Linda tremble each time his fingers brushed against her skin. He freed the last button and stepped back. Linda shrugged her shoulders, and with a twist of her body her dress and slip slid down. She stood in the moonlight wearing only a pair of knee-length pantalettes, her breasts rising and falling as the tempo of her breathing increased.

"Hurry, Ki!" she urged. "You haven't taken off anything at all yet!"

"But I don't have so many buttons to undo," Ki said.

He was already shedding his vest, and while Linda was stripping off her pantalettes, he opened his belt and let his trousers fall. When Linda looked up, he was wearing only his *cache-sexe,* a broad cotton band wrapped around his waist and brought up under his crotch.

Ki had not been with a woman for many weeks, and the sight of Linda standing naked, the tips of her heavy breasts budding in the cool air, her satiny thighs glowing in the moonlight, set his desire to stirring. He brought his hand up to pull away the *cache-sexe,* but Linda spoke quickly.

"Wait, Ki. Let me."

Ki had not allowed himself to become fully aroused, but when Linda groped for the tucked end of the cloth band and finally pulled it away, she looked at him and gasped.

"Oh, my!" she breathed, letting the cloth strip fall and cradling his swelling sword in her palms. "Are all Japanese men so big?"

Ki did not reply. He'd lowered his head to Linda's breasts and was caressing them with his lips and tongue. She moaned, a soft sound deep in her throat like the purring of a giant cat, then started rolling her shoulders from side to side. Arching her back, she tucked Ki's burgeoning sword be-

35

tween her thighs. With his shaft cradled in the warmth of her soft flesh, Ki allowed it to swell until it was firm and fully erect. Linda gasped and began trembling.

"I want you in me, Ki!" she cried. "Now! Hurry, please!"

Ki did not make her wait. Without interrupting the caresses he was lavishing on the firm tips of her heaving breasts, he put a hand under each of Linda's knees and lifted her, spreading her thighs as he brought her upward. She wriggled her hips and reached down to position his swollen shaft, locked her legs around his hips, and drew him into her hot, wet depths.

"Oh, wonderful!" she sighed. "Nobody's ever filled me up this way before! Now, go on, Ki! Hurry! I feel I'm going to explode any minute!"

Ki cradled her soft buttocks in his clasped hands and began thrusting, holding Linda suspended as he moved his hips slowly back and forth, pulling her to him with a quick, hard jerk at the end of each stroke. She dropped her head to his sinewy shoulder and nibbled at his smooth skin until she was caught up in a trembling that she tried to control but could not.

"Faster, Ki!" she urged. "I'm— I'm— Oh, Ki! Now, hold me! Hold me!"

Her moans ended in an ecstatic scream as her body trembled and her hips writhed from side to side. Ki slowed the tempo of his thrusting, but did not stop completely. Linda threw her head back, and her cries reached a crescendo as her ecstasy crested, then passed and began to ebb. Slowly her taut muscles relaxed. Ki slowed his stroking to a gentler pace until she sighed contentedly and let her head drop back limply to his shoulder.

"Oh, that was wonderful, Ki," she breathed. "And I don't know how you do it, but you're still as big and hard as ever. Didn't you—"

"Not yet," Ki broke in. "We're just starting, Linda."

"But you must be tired of holding me up."

"You're not all that heavy. But maybe we would be more comfortable in the bottom of the wagon bed."

Still holding himself buried in her warm depths, Ki lowered Linda to her back in the bed of the wagon. Then, without waiting, he began thrusting again, this time in a quicker rhythm. He plunged with full, strong strokes that sent his hard shaft deeper than before and soon brought Linda to her crest and over it.

Ki did not pause as she passed, trembling and crying out with ecstasy, through the plateau of her delight. Instead, though Linda grew limp after her peak had passed, he kept up his driving thrusts until she again started quivering and tossing, supreme pleasure and pleasant pain mingling in the formless cries from her throat. Suddenly Ki drove faster and deeper than before, rising to his own peak in an explosion that tore through them both.

Moments passed as they rested in each other's arms. Linda gave a soft, contented sigh as she nuzzled her face into Ki's chest. "I never dreamed there was anything like this," she whispered. "And every time I expected you to stop, you just started over again. But I guess we'd better get up now, or I'll miss my train."

"Not yet," Ki said. "There's plenty of time, unless you're too tired and want to—"

"No!" Linda broke in. "I don't want to stop, ever! And you know something, Ki? I don't really care whether I miss that train or not, as long as you can make me feel the way I do now."

Chapter 4

Alone in the main house of the Circle Star, Jessie curled up in her favorite chair. It was the big leather armchair that had been her father's, and often when she nestled into its deep springy cushions, Jessie was sure she could still catch a hint of Alex's pipe tobacco.

She leaned back and closed her eyes, glad to be back in the study with its huge stone fireplace and the oil painting of her long-dead mother dominating the room from its familiar place on the wall opposite the door. Dusk was setting in and the room was becoming shadowed, but Jessie did not light a lamp. The dimness was as welcome to her as the silence of the big room.

Though the Box B had been much quieter after Linda's departure, Jessie had still borne the strain of constantly nursing Brad Close. Her biggest job came after the old rancher had recovered enough to get out of bed. At that point, despite the fact that he was still weak and tottery, Brad had announced to Jessie and the hands that he was a well man once more. All of Jessie's patience, as well as an occasional scolding and the expenditure of a considerable amount of energy, had been required to keep him from mounting up and taking charge of his ranch again.

When she at last considered him fit enough to be left to Hardrock's attention, Jessie and Ki had returned to the Circle Star. It was while they were riding home that Jessie voiced the uneasy thoughts that had occurred to her earlier.

"Ki," she'd said, "if the cartel's been trying to buy the Box B, don't you think they'd also be after the other ranches that border the Circle Star?"

"That hadn't occurred to me," Ki replied. "But it's something we can find out very quickly. Suppose I should ride over to the Cross Spikes and the Lazy G and ask a few questions?"

"I think that would be a very good way to spend the next two days," Jessie agreed. "You can't cover them both in a single day, but if you swing around from the Cross Spikes to the G, you can make it home in a beeline."

Ki had insisted on starting on his errand as soon as they'd gotten back. He'd left the previous afternoon, and Jessie had used the time alone to dispose of the large heap of mail that Ed Wright had brought from the whistle-stop during her absence. The letters lay in neat piles on the long table that stood beside Alex's scarred rolltop desk across the room.

Going through the mail had been a time-consuming job, even though most of the letters were nothing more than routine reports from the different businesses that made up the far-flung industrial empire that Alex Starbuck had spent so many years in putting together. From his modest start in a small shop in San Francisco where he'd dealt in second-hand merchandise and a few objects imported from the Far East, Jessie's father had created a vast industrial complex.

As his import business prospered, Alex had bought a battered sailing ship to carry merchandise from Japan and

China to the United States. He'd soon added a second vessel to the first, and from there on his progress had been steady. The two ships had grown into a modest fleet of merchant freighters serving the increasing trade between the U.S. and the Orient, and his success with the fleet had led Alex to begin building merchantmen.

At the beginning of the era of iron ships, he'd been among the first to convert his small shipyard to making iron-hulled steamers, and this had led to his setting up his own steel mill, as well as to buying mines to supply the mill with ores. When the railroads burst on the scene, Alex's mills began rolling out rails, and plate for locomotive boilers. Realizing the giant potential of the railroads, he had also begun buying railroad stock just as the boom began. As his investments prospered and his industrial holdings grew larger, he'd needed ready financing, which led him into banking, and from banking to brokerage.

Alex Starbuck's meteoric rise had drawn the attention not only of the nation's long-established industrial and financial giants. The masters of a large European cartel had noticed him as well. Alex was invited to bring his industries into the cartel, but when he discovered that the group's secret objective was to gain control of the full industrial might of the United States, his patriotism had led him to refuse. From that time on, an undeclared war had raged between him and the ring of unscrupulous financiers who were the cartel's secret masters.

When the cartel's hired killers cut down Alex in a surprise raid on the Circle Star—the ranch he'd bought as an isolated haven where he could enjoy rest and peace—Alex's empire had passed on to Jessie, who was his only heir. Jessie's mother had died in childbirth.

Even before Alex's marriage and Jessie's birth, Ki had joined him. Ki came from the family of a Japanese samurai who had disowned Ki's mother for taking an American husband. Ki had been Alex's confidential aide as well as his friend and confidant, and he continued to serve Jessie in that same role.

Loving the Circle Star as much as her father had, Jessie continued to think of the ranch not only as a base of operations for the Starbuck industries, but as her home and haven. She and Ki traveled now and then to check on the operations of the Starbuck holdings, but as much as possible Jessie handled her business affairs by mail.

She'd become accustomed to receiving reports, financial statements, all the minute details, in correspondence that piled up in heaps during her absence from the ranch, as had the letters she now looked at on the table in the study. Jessie thought now of the single letter she had put aside. She was starting to get out of the big chair to reread it when the sound of the front door reached her ears, followed by Ki's call.

"Jessie? Are you in the study?"

Sinking back in her comfortable seat, she replied, "Yes, Ki. Come on in."

Ki joined her, settling on the low divan that sat at right angles to her chair. He said, "Your hunch was right, Jessie."

"It's the cartel's operating pattern showing up again?"

"Yes."

"Go on," she said. "Tell me the details."

"There's not much to tell. After I'd passed the time of day with George Brady at the Cross Spikes, talking about cattle and the weather for a few minutes, I asked him if anybody's been trying to buy his spread."

"And had they?"

"Yes, just as you suspected. George took me into his office and showed me a letter from a cattle broker in San

Antonio. The broker said he knew someone who was interested in buying the Spikes and asked George to set a price on the spread. Then he showed me a copy of the letter he'd sent the broker. It was only five words long. 'Not interested, now or ever.'"

Jessie nodded. "I was pretty sure George is satisfied with the Spikes. He's a solid rancher; he knows what he has there. What about the Lazy G?"

"Well, you remember the run-in I had a while back with those Lazy G hands who were trying to have a lynching party?"

"Of course I do."

"So does Bob Manners, and it still rankles him."

"But he didn't throw you off the place?"

"No. He seems to be getting over that grudge. He even offered me a bed in the main house instead of the bunkhouse when I rode in just before supper. He didn't invite me to eat with him, though. I ate in the bunkhouse dining room with the hands."

"And did you sleep in the main house?"

Smiling, Ki shook his head. "No. I stayed in the bunkhouse. But at least he didn't refuse to talk to me, the way he did for quite a while."

"And had he gotten an offer too?"

"Of course. Only this one was from a bank in Fort Worth. They said one of their correspondent banks in San Francisco has a party who's looking for a large ranch in this part of Texas."

"Did Manners show you the letter?"

"No. Somehow he'd jumped to the conclusion that you were the one behind the offer. The first question he asked me was if you were trying to buy him out."

Jessie frowned. "Why would I get a bank in San Francisco to send him an offer by mail? If I wanted to talk to him about buying the Lazy G, Manners ought to know I'd just ride over and talk to him myself."

"*You* know that's what you'd do, Jessie, and so do I. But Manners is distrustful by nature. He's always sure that someone is trying to put something over on him."

"Yes, that's what several cattle brokers have told me. And I don't suppose Manners will ever admit that any woman is bright enough to run a cattle ranch."

"Well, I finally convinced him that you'd heard there've been some offers made to buy ranches in this part of Texas, and just wanted to make sure."

"Did he loosen up after that?"

"A little bit," Ki answered. "Not enough to show me the letter, but enough to tell me very positively that he couldn't be persuaded to sell the Lazy G to anybody for any price."

Jessie nodded and sat silently thoughtful for a moment or two. Then she said, "It's a typical cartel pattern, Ki. I'm sure it's not just a coincidence that the owners of all three of the ranches adjoining the Circle Star got those offers about the same time. And the only buyer who showed his face was the one who approached Brad Close."

"I don't think you've got anything to worry about, Jessie. All three of the offers were refused, so it's not likely we'll have a cartel operation next to the Circle Star."

"Even if they've failed this time, they're not going to stop trying," she pointed out.

"Of course not. But you're the one who figured out the way the cartel always reacts when one of their schemes fails. They pull in their horns and let us alone for a while."

"Yes," Jessie agreed. "And I'm sure that's what they'll do this time, especially since they lost one of their hired killers trying to murder Brad."

"I get the idea you're trying to convince yourself to do something, Jessie," Ki said. "Something you'd like to do, but can't quite justify."

"You know me almost as well as I know myself, Ki," Jessie said with a smile. "You're right, of course."

"Why don't you tell me about it," Ki suggested.

"While you were gone, I went through the mail that had piled up while we were at the Box B," she said. "There was one letter that—well, it doesn't have anything at all to do with business, or the cartel, or anything except a personal friendship."

"And you're like Alex. You follow the same rules he did," Ki said. "And his first rule was never to let his personal life interfere with business."

"Alex's rules have worked as well for me as they did for him," Jessie pointed out.

"Of course. But he gave up a great deal for those rules. I think you have, too."

"If I have, I haven't begrudged it, Ki," she said. "This time, though . . ." Jessie stood up and went to the table where the piles of mail were stacked, and picked up the letter she'd set aside. She went on, "This is from a girl I knew in finishing school. You remember, the one in the East that Alex sent me to a couple of years before his death."

"I remember quite well." Ki smiled. "Miss Booth's Academy and School of Deportment for Selected Female Students. The name always fascinated me."

"Well, the school didn't fascinate me," Jessie said, her voice chilly. "I was miserable there after having spent most of my time out here in the West. It was full of nasty little snobbish cliques. The girls from Boston and Philadelphia all came from families that had inherited money and social position, and they looked down on the girls from New York

44

and other places, whose fathers were self-made men. There was a lot of backbiting and cutting little remarks, and— Well, it just wasn't a nice place."

"I know your letters used to bother Alex," Ki said.

"Really? But I was so careful not to say anything in them that would even hint at how I felt!"

"He could read between the lines, Jessie. But he was determined to see that you knew what he called 'the social graces.'"

"Oh, I learned how to pour tea and what silver went where on a formal dinner table," Jessie said. "And a lot of other things that I suppose are useful now and then. But I didn't belong in either the social-snob group or the Eastern-business group. In fact, Teresa and I were pretty much by ourselves."

"Teresa?"

"Teresa Maria Angelina Lucia Velarde y Lozano," Jessie said, smiling.

"With a name like that, obviously your friend is a genuine aristocrat," Ki chuckled.

"From a very old New Mexico family. The Velarde family came to this country with the first emigrants from Spain. They received a royal land grant of—well, I don't know how many thousand acres—in New Mexico, which was New Spain then, of course. And because she was Spanish by birth, the little snobs at Miss Booth's treated her like an outcast, just as they did me."

"That must've given you a great deal in common."

"It did, Ki, even though she was a lot younger than I was. We were going to keep in touch after we left school, but so many things happened to me—Alex's death, and everything that's followed. We did write fairly regularly at first, but that tapered off when I got so busy. It's been years since we've heard from one another, but there was this letter from her waiting in the mail when we got back from the Box B."

"Let me guess," Ki said. "She's invited you to visit her, and you'd like to go."

"Yes, I would like to visit her. Not just because I want to see her again, but because I can read between the lines of this letter. Teresa badly needs some advice and maybe some help."

"What kind of help?"

"I'm not sure. Since I got the letter, I've been trying to remember things Teresa told me about some sort of feud or vendetta that's been going on for years between her family and another family in the area where she lives."

"I don't even know where that is, Jessie," Ki broke in.

"It's up in northern New Mexico, above Santa Fe. Teresa called it the Rio Arriba, which means upper river, but I'm not exactly sure what river it's applied to or where it is."

"I suppose it'd have to be the Rio Grande," Ki said thoughtfully. "It's New Mexico's main river, and if I remember my geography, its headwaters are up in the Rocky Mountains, in Colorado somewhere."

"Wherever it is, I got the impression from the way Teresa described it that the country's wild, almost primitive. The land was parceled out in huge sections by the king of Spain as a way to get some of the noble families to settle there."

"How long ago was that, Jessie?"

"About a hundred years before the Pilgrims landed," Jessie replied. "Teresa mentioned once that the land her family owns was granted to them around 1550."

"And it's still wild, primitive country?"

"That's what Teresa told me, Ki. I've never been there. Northern New Mexico is one of the few places where Alex never developed any kind of business interest."

46

"I suppose there wasn't much to develop," Ki remarked.

"From the way Teresa talked, I got the idea that the old Spanish noblemen who got those big land grants were very jealous people. They didn't want a lot of outsiders—especially Anglo-Saxons—getting any kind of hold on their land."

"Sounds like you and your friend from Miss Booth's used to do a lot of talking. I get the idea you'd like to see her again."

Jessie was silent for a moment; then she said, "I would, Ki. Very much indeed. I've thought of her now and then, but since Alex's death I haven't had time to do anything much except keep the cartel from taking over the businesses he worked so hard to develop."

"Yes, the cartel's kept us busy," Ki agreed. Then he went on, "But we were talking a few minutes ago about the pattern they seem to follow, Jessie. Unless we're both wrong, they should pull in their horns now for several months while they try to find a new point of attack."

"It's what they've always done in the past."

"I don't see any reason why you shouldn't do what you want to for the next couple of months, then."

"I've just about convinced myself of the same thing."

"You're going to visit your friend?"

"Yes, Ki. Nothing urgent's going to need my attention for a few weeks, so as soon as we can pack, we'll leave for New Mexico. I'll enjoy the rest as well as having my visit with Teresa."

Chapter 5

Because the gnarled, ground-hugging piñon trees that crowded the slope rarely grew higher than eye level, all that Jessie and Ki could see from their saddles were the tops of the low-growing pines against the sunset-tinged sky. After four days on the trail, they'd learned to let the horses have free rein. They made little effort to guide the sturdy little animals now, but let them pick their own way across the deep gullies that had been cut by melting snow and washed still deeper by the sudden slashing rains that often raged so furiously in that more-than-mile-high country.

They'd rented the small, mountain-wise ponies at the livery stable maintained by La Fonda Hotel in Santa Fe, where they'd stopped overnight to rest after an almost sleepless three-day train trip from the Circle Star. Since leaving New Mexico's capital city their progress had been slow, most of it uphill, on narrow roads beaten across the rocky red ground by more than two centuries of use.

The path they were following now couldn't really be called a road, Jessie thought, even though she could see the wheel tracks left by wagons and by the square, low-slung, two-wheeled *carretas,* which were the most popular local means of transportation. The dusty surface also showed the sharply incised tracks of horses, the flatter prints of mule hooves, the dainty pocks made by the tiny feet of mountain burros, and the even tinier dimples of the delicate feet of deer. She noted that the dust bore no human footprints.

"I wish those people in the villages we've passed through since Santa Fe had been a little bit more helpful about giving us directions," Ki remarked, as though he'd been catching Jessie's thought. Then he reached for the reins as his horse stumbled on the loose stones underfoot.

"Teresa told me once that a lot of the people up here don't get more than a few miles from their home villages during their entire lifetimes," Jessie said. "I didn't really believe her at the time, but I certainly do now."

"I'm getting to the point where I'd believe almost anything I was told about this Rio Arriba country," Ki said. "It certainly isn't like anyplace we've ever been before."

"I think I have to agree with you, Ki," Jessie replied. "Nobody seems to know where anything but their own homes are located, and they don't even seem to *want* to know."

Jessie and Ki had been surprised to find English virtually an unknown language after they'd traveled a very few miles north from Santa Fe. In Pojoaque and Chimayo, the first villages where they'd stopped overnight, the residents had been able to understand the Mexican border Spanish of which both Ki and Jessie had a marginal command.

At their first night's stop, in Pojoaque, only a score of miles from Santa Fe, they'd had no trouble at all in establishing communication with the local people, even though the accents and some of their words had been unfamiliar. There'd even been two or three of the younger villagers who could understand a few simple words and phrases in English.

In Chimayo the next night, there had been gaps. The local Spanish accent was heavily influenced by the Pueblo tongue and had strange words that were unintelligible to Jessie and Ki. The villagers had just as much trouble with Jessie and Ki's border Spanish, which was heavily influenced not only by English but by the Mayan and Aztec tongues. Still, the gaps had been spanned, and the travelers had been sure they were on the right road when they started north from Chimayo.

The next night, at a village smaller than either of the first two, whose name neither Jessie nor Ki were certain they'd understood, the language barrier had proved almost insurmountable. Both travelers and villagers tried, but they found too many differences in their words and accents to speak fluently to one another. The local residents seemed as vague about the roads leading to the Rancho Velarde as Jessie and Ki were themselves. They had obviously heard of the rancho, for they nodded and smiled when she or Ki mentioned the Velarde name, but when asked for directions they only bobbed their heads again and gestured in a generally northward direction.

There was only one road leading northward out of the last village, and Jessie and Ki had started over it at dawn. Shortly before noon they'd reached a fork, but after consulting the map Jessie had tucked into her saddlebag, they were still unable to decide which branch led where. The tracks showed that both of the roads seemed to carry the same amount of traffic, and at last they'd chosen to follow the one that ran most directly northward.

"It's too bad this map doesn't show where the different ranches are," Jessie said. "And I suppose it's my fault that I didn't write Teresa and get exact directions. But when we asked about the roads at the livery stable in Santa Fe, the man said all we had to do was keep traveling north and we'd find the Rancho Velarde without any trouble."

"Oh, it's nobody's fault," Ki told her. "And if your friend's place is as big as she told you, we might even be on it now. Aside from those short stone fences in the villages, we haven't seen any signs of property lines since we've been on the road north."

"Different countries, different customs." Jessie shrugged. "But I'd hate to think of trying to run cattle up here the way we do back home. Can you imagine the range disputes we'd have with neighbors like Bob Manners if we didn't have barbwire around the boundaries of the Circle Star?"

Ahead of them, the raucous shrilling of a jay shattered the stillness. Before the rasping birdcall had died away, a rifle barked, its report flattened by the thin air. The slug whined between them, and in instinctive reaction both Jessie and Ki dropped from their horses. As their feet hit the ground, they slid their own rifles from their saddle holsters before dropping flat on the red earth beside the trail and rolling into the cover of the low-hanging piñon branches.

"Did you see anybody?" Jessie asked after they'd lain still for a few seconds. She pitched her voice to a half whisper, loud enough to be heard by Ki but inaudible a dozen yards away.

"No. But whoever did the shooting spooked that jay that squawked just before the shot sounded," he replied.

A second shot broke the stillness and the slug sang through the low pinyons behind them, cutting through a few small branches with a high-pitched thunking sound. Their horses were still standing in the narrow trail and one of them whickered uneasily, but neither of the animals moved.

"Whoever it is can't see us," Ki volunteered. "They're shooting way too high."

"I don't think they're trying to hit us, Ki," Jessie said. "They're just warning us that we're heading someplace where they don't want us to go."

"Maybe they use rifles instead of fences up here to keep their property lines secure," Ki suggested.

"Well, it's certainly not a way I'd like to use," Jessie said tartly. "I'm beginning to think this trip wasn't such a good idea, Ki."

Even though Jessie had spoken softly, the invisible sniper must have heard her voice, for a third shot broke the air and the bullet whistled high over their heads. This time, it did not even cut through the thin piñon stand.

"What do we do, then?" Ki asked. "It's getting dark, and we haven't any idea how much further we've got to go."

"I don't think there's much we can do," Jessie replied. "I don't want to return their fire. That might only make things worse."

"It's a Mexican—maybe I ought to say a *New* Mexican— standoff then," Ki remarked wryly. "We can't see whoever it is that's shooting at us, he doesn't seem interested in hitting us, and we don't want to shoot back."

"I guess that sums it up as well as anything can," Jessie agreed. "It seems to me the best thing we can do is nothing."

"But why us?" Ki asked. "We're strangers up here."

"That might be the reason. The people up here might figure that they already know all their friends, and any stranger who shows up must be an enemy."

"I don't like the idea of being shot at without shooting back," Ki said. "Even if those were only warning shots."

"I don't like it either," she agreed. "But if that sniper intended to hit us, he had plenty of time to get us in his sights before he shot."

Night was coming swiftly now, the quick darkness of

high altitudes chopping off their view of the peaks that towered to the east, while the pinnacles to the west were still silhouetted against the dropping sun. Already the stars were showing in the eastern sky, and the full moon that had seemed only a pale circle before sunset was beginning to glow. Its light was as cold as the fitful, chilly wind that was beginning to make itself felt as the sun's rays left the sky.

"I think the bushwhacker's gone," Ki said after minutes had ticked off with no more shots. "I'll see if I can find out." He lifted his rifle muzzle and triggered off a shot into the darkening sky. No replying shot sounded, and after waiting a few moments more, he went on, "Keep watching for movement in that brush ahead of us, Jessie. I'm going to try test number two."

With his lithe, muscular body tensed to react at once, Ki rose to his feet. No shots greeted him. He stepped cautiously onto the trail where the horses still waited, but the evening silence remained unbroken.

Jessie rose from the ground and joined him. She said, "I don't know what to make of it, Ki. When Teresa and I were at school together and she was telling me about this Rio Arriba country, she said the people up here were always carrying on some long-standing feuds, but she never did mention this kind of indiscriminate shooting."

"If what we just had was a sample of the way they greet strangers up here in the daytime, I'd hate to run into somebody in the dark," Ki told her. "Don't you think we'd better make camp right here, and wait until daylight to find the Velarde ranch?"

"I certainly do," Jessie agreed. "Let's look for a place where we'll be sheltered, though. That breeze is cold."

Leading their horses, Jessie and Ki followed the upslope trail until they reached a small arroyo, then turned up the little gully until they found a place where it widened out.

53

Jessie stopped and looked around, her eyes now accustomed to the moonlit gloom. She said, "I suppose this is about as good a place as we'll find in the dark, even if it does mean a dry camp tonight."

"We have enough water in our canteens," Ki replied. "And the horses can get by until we run across a creek or some kind of water hole in the morning. But let me scramble up to the ridge and take a look at what's ahead. The moonlight's bright enough for me to see a little way. We might even be close enough to the ranch house to see lights from its windows."

He mounted the steep slope quickly. On the rim of the arroyo the chill night breeze cut through his trail garb as his sharp eyes searched ahead through the moonlight. Its bluish hue turned the sparse foliage of the piñons to black, and the reddish earth to a dark purple.

It was an unreal landscape he gazed at, one of stark, violent contrasts but beautiful in an unearthly fashion. There were no signs of human habitation visible, nor did he see the glint of water throwing back the moonlight. After he'd scanned the terrain in all directions, he slid back to the floor of the gully.

"Nothing," he told Jessie. "We might as well stay where we are."

Working with the quick efficiency born of having pitched many camps in many places, Jessie and Ki hitched the horses, then took their blankets and saddlebags off the cantles before unsaddling the animals. They worked in silence. No words were needed between them; they'd shared so many camps together that they could communicate without conversation at such times.

Eventually Jessie broke the silence. "I don't think it'd be wise to build a fire."

"Definitely not," Ki agreed. "The chances are that nobody will come prowling around now that the sniper seems to have left, but there's no need to take an extra risk."

"If I'd thought there was a chance we wouldn't find the Velarde ranch before dark, I'd have bought something besides those tortillas at the place where we stopped last night."

"It's not your fault, Jessie," Ki told her consolingly. "And we've been on short rations before."

Their bedrolls spread, Jessie and Ki hunkered down and pulled their blankets around their shoulders. The thin night breeze was blowing steadily now, washing past their faces like a stream of icy water. Jessie took the tortillas from her saddlebag and passed two of them to Ki. These were not the thin, tender cornmeal tortillas they were accustomed to, but were thick and crusty, made of flour, and took a lot of chewing before they could be swallowed.

"I feel like a foolish tenderfoot," Jessie said between bites. "Not bringing a better map, not getting better directions where we stopped last night. I suppose the idea of a vacation just made me careless."

"That's natural enough," Ki told her. "You haven't made a trip that wasn't for business in more years than I can remember."

"I suppose it has been a long time," she agreed. "And I didn't want to put off starting, so all I told Teresa in the note I sent her was that we were coming. I didn't even consider asking her for directions. From what she's said, it's such a big spread that I just assumed anybody could tell us how to get to it."

"Cheer up, Jessie," Ki said. "It's not your fault. I'm sure we won't have any trouble finding the Velarde place tomorrow. We should be close enough to it by now."

"Yes. I suppose that road we've been following must lead somewhere. All we've got to do—" She stopped short as Ki raised his hand and gestured for silence.

55

In the dead quiet, the soft sighing of the wind sounded like a distant humming. Then Jessie heard the branches of the pinyons rustling faintly, but in a fashion that could not have been caused by the breeze. She saw Ki's arm move as he slid a *shuriken* from a vest pocket, and she drew her Colt from its holster. The low-branched trees at the rim of the draw rustled again, and both she and Ki swiveled their heads slowly, their eyes probing the shadows below the low-growing trees as they searched for the source of the sound.

Ki broke their silence with a chuckle. "It's all right, Jessie," he said. "It's just a deer."

"I still don't see it."

"You're looking too far to your left. Watch that patch of shadow about twenty feet to our right, on the rim."

Reaching to the ground, Ki picked up a stone and tossed it. Jessie got a glimpse of blurred motion as the deer leaped out of the tree's deep shadow and bounded off on stiltlike legs into the night.

"At least we won't have to worry about standing watch," he said. "With that deer wandering around peacefully, I think its safe to assume that nobody's prowling around anywhere close to us now."

"Yes, their senses are a lot keener than ours," Jessie agreed. "And I feel about ready to go to sleep. Riding that little pony in these mountains certainly isn't as restful as riding Sun on the prairie back home."

"I think it might even be safe to build a fire after all, if you're cold," Ki suggested. "It's not likely a little blaze would be seen down here in the arroyo."

"Don't bother, Ki," she said. "It isn't all that cold. Our blankets ought to keep us warm enough."

"Whatever you say," he replied. "And I feel about like you do, ready to go to sleep."

Rearranging their bedrolls, they pulled the heavy warm

blankets up around their shoulders and tucked them in well to keep out any chilling drafts. Within minutes, both Jessie and Ki were sleeping soundly.

At some time later in the night, Jessie woke. She opened her eyes suddenly, and by habit her hand moved to the butt of her Colt, which lay holstered at her side. Other than the silent gliding of her hand to the gun, she did not move.

While she'd slept, the moon had dropped below the ridge, and the bed of the arroyo was an impenetrable black. She could see a few stars in the gaps between the foliage, but the faint starlight was not bright enough to reveal any details of her surroundings.

She could feel the butt of the Colt pressing against her fingers and closed her hand around it. As the moments ticked away and no sound broke the stillness, Jessie relaxed again. Closing her eyes, she went to sleep once more.

When Jessie opened her eyes again, it was gray dawn. Glancing at Ki's bedroll, she saw that he was still asleep. Then a flick of motion on the bank of the arroyo caught her eye. Jessie turned her head to look, and found herself staring into the menacing black muzzle of a rifle held by a roughly dressed man who sat propped against a tree a half-dozen yards away.

Chapter 6

"All right, lady," said the thickset man holding the rifle. "Just stay still, and you won't get hurt."

"Who are you?" Jessie demanded.

Aroused by the voices, Ki sat up in his blankets and began turning to look around. Before he'd moved more than a few inches, the stranger snapped, "You, mister! Don't you move, either! I ain't anxious to hurt you or your lady friend, but don't think for a minute I won't shoot if you start anything!"

"Who are you?" Jessie repeated.

She'd thought of drawing her Colt when the man turned his attention to Ki, but a quick second thought had wiped out the idea. Now, he was looking back at her again, his rifle held rock steady. Jessie reminded herself that for all she knew, the stranger might be an official of some kind, with the right to question trespassers. He might even be employed by the Velardes as a guard for their ranch. She gave up the idea of using the Colt until she'd learned more about the situation.

"That's neither here nor there," the man replied. "Far as you two are concerned, I'm the one that's holding the gun, and I'll tell you right off that it's got a hair trigger. Now, that's all you'll know till you tell me who you are and what you're doing here!"

"My name is Jessica Starbuck," Jessie replied. "This is my companion. His name is Ki."

When the stranger heard the odd-sounding name, he took his eyes off Jessie long enough to focus them on Ki for the first time.

"Well, billy-be-damned!" he exclaimed. "Your skin ain't dark enough for you to be Indian, so I guess you're a Chinee."

"Japanese," Ki replied. "And we're not here to harm anyone."

"Just what are you here for, then?" the man asked.

Jessie said quickly, "We're on our way to visit friends. We must've taken the wrong turn at that fork a few miles back, because we wound up here in the dark. Instead of trying to go on in the darkness, and getting lost worse then we were, we stopped for the night."

"I guess you know the name of these friends you say you're looking for?" the stranger went on.

"Of course I do!" Jessie replied. "Velarde." When she saw the man's jaw muscles bulge and his mouth compress into a thin line at her mention of the name, she explained quickly, "Teresa Velarde and I went to school together back east, quite some time ago. I haven't seen her for years, but she invited me to visit her at her grandfather's ranch. I imagine it's around here somewhere."

"You ain't been to the Velarde place before?" he asked.

Jessie shook her head. "No."

"And you don't know any of 'em but this girl, Teresa?"

"No," she repeated. Then, deciding she'd answered

enough questions, she asked the rifleman, "What gives you the right to question us? Are you an officer of the law?"

"Not likely! Now, you might be who you say you are, but if you're heading for the Velarde place, you sure taken the wrong road to get to it. That makes me a mite suspicious, so I aim to take you along to where there's others that'll have some questions I maybe can't think to ask you."

Ki broke in to ask, "What right do you have to force us to go with you? You say you're not an officer."

His face still set grimly, the stranger patted the stock of his rifle. "This here's all the law I need, Chink."

"My name is Ki," Ki told him. "And I'm not sure we'll go anywhere with you."

"Let's don't argue with him, Ki," Jessie said quickly. "We haven't anything to hide or to be afraid of. We'll go with him and see if we can't straighten things out." She turned to the stranger. "I guess you won't mind if we gather up our gear and take it along with us?"

"Go ahead," he said, nodding. "Load it on your horses. You can lead 'em. It ain't far where we're heading."

"Just where are we heading?" Ki asked as he stepped out of his blankets. He stooped down and began to bundle them up.

"Big Piney," the stranger replied.

Ki was covertly watching Jessie as she bent down to her bedroll. He said, "That doesn't mean much to a couple of strangers. Exactly what is Big Piney? A town, a ranch?"

Before the stranger could reply, Jessie whirled up from her blankets, her Colt leveled. Ki had been poised on his haunches waiting for her to turn. He launched himself at the stranger in an arcing leap that covered the distance between them before the man could swing the muzzle of his rifle around.

While Ki was still in midair, Jessie fired a shot into the

ground. The slug kicked up dirt in the few inches of space between the man's booted toes. The spurt of dust raised by the Colt's slug further distracted the man, whose eyes had been fixed on Ki's body hurtling toward him.

Totally confused by the explosion of a joint attack from people he'd begun to think of as harmless, the stranger triggered his rifle without aiming just as Ki landed a *te-gatana* blow with the iron-hard muscles in the edge of his tensed hand. The blow caught the man's forearm and sent the muzzle of his rifle upward. The rifle bullet sailed harmlessly into the sky.

Ki used the impetus of the weapon's recoil to wrest the weapon from its owner. As Ki whirled away, he gained enough distance to cover the man with his own rifle. For a moment the man stood motionless in slack-jawed amazement, looking from Ki to Jessie and back to Ki again.

"What kinda people are you, anyhow?" he asked at last. "I never seen tricks like you pulled outside of a circus!"

"This isn't a circus," Jessie told him sternly. "Now it's your turn to do a little explaining. You might start by telling us your name."

"Looks like I ain't got much choice, don't it?" The man grinned ruefully. "Guess I better tell you. The way you two turned the tables on me, I ain't about to push you too far. My name's Mike Burns, and I live at Big Piney."

"Suppose you tell us what Big Piney is, and where it's located," Jessie went on. "Remember, we don't know this part of the country."

"Why, Big Piney's mostly just some houses and a saw-mill, about two miles from here," Burns explained. He frowned and went on, "If you'd kept on the road instead of turning off to shelter in the arroyo, you'd have seen our lights soon as you got to the top of the rise."

"Big Piney's a town?" Jessie asked.

61

"It ain't big enough to be called a town, lady, not even in the Rio Arriba. Like I said, it's a sawmill and some houses."

"You're a lumberman, then," Ki said.

"That's right." Burns nodded. "Only we're getting sorta short on meat, so I come out this morning to see could I spook up a deer. Making lumber's hungry work."

"Is your mill part of the Velarde ranch?" Jessie asked.

"It sure as hell ain't, lady!" Burns said. "Begging your pardon for the cussing. It's on land we bought from old Don Esteban Velarde when we first come here from the States, and if you know them Velardes you can tell 'em we ain't about to back away from fighting to keep it!"

"I've already told you that the only member of the Velarde family I know is Teresa, Don Esteban's granddaughter," Jessie reminded him. "And if you're having any kind of dispute with her family over land they sold you or you squatted on, I don't want to get involved in it." She turned to Ki. "Let's reserve judgment on Mr. Burns, Ki. Hold on to his rifle, and just in case you might need to use it, I imagine he's carrying some spare shells that you might like to take away from him."

Burns said quickly, "Begging your pardon, Miss—Starbuck, did you say your name was?" When Jessie nodded, he went on, "If you'll take my word that I don't hold no hard feelings toward you, and won't do you no harm, I can maybe help you."

"In return for what?" Jessie asked.

"For giving me back my rifle and not taking what few shells I got in my pocket. Powder and lead's mighty hard to come by here, and we're running low on both of 'em at Big Piney."

"What do we get in return?"

"If you're strangers like you say you are, there's a lot of

things about the Rio Arriba you'll need to know," Burns said quickly. "I can maybe save you a lot of trouble."

"Trouble's the last thing we're looking for," Jessie told him. "I'll make you a bargain, Mr. Burns. Ki will carry your rifle and you can keep the shells in your pocket. I'll make up my mind after we've found out a little bit more about you and your friends, and if I'm satisfied, we'll return your rifle."

"You look and talk like a lady whose word's good," Burns replied after a moment's thought. "We got a deal."

Within a few minutes, Ki had saddled the horses and put their bedrolls and saddlebags in place, and they moved along the bottom of the arroyo to the road. When they reached the crest of the rise and looked down from it into a shallow broad valley, Jessie had the feeling that they were leaving one world and entering another, so dramatically did the character of the country change.

Just below the ridge crest, the piñon forest began to thin out, the stunted-looking little trees giving way to towering pines. As far as they could see down the valley's sloping sides, the tall conifers stood thick, an uncut virgin forest. At the bottom of the slope they could see a sizable river winding its gentle, serpentine course.

In the distance they saw another, smaller stream that joined the first, and a mile or more below the vee where the two streams met, great heaps of huge boulders spanned the flow to create a natural dam. The sparkling water had spread out behind the boulders to form a good-sized lake, and along one section of its shore a half-dozen log cabins were scattered over a wide crescent. On the near side of the settlement stood the stumps of the trees that had been felled to build the cabins; another, much larger log structure sat at the edge of the lake. Jessie assumed that the large building was the sawmill.

"That's Big Piney?" she asked.

"Sure is," Burns replied. "A'course, that ain't all of it. The sawmill hides the millrace and the log pond, and there's a few more cabins you can't see from here for the trees."

"Aren't there any people down there?" Ki asked. "If there are, I don't see them."

"Oh, they're there, all right," Burns assured him. "But the men're either out felling or in the mill, and this is the time of day when the womenfolks clean house."

They started down the long gentle slope, and the thick pine forest hid the settlement from sight as they descended. A bit more than halfway down the saucerlike valley the trail forked, and Ki said to Burns, "I guess that right-hand fork leads to your mill and houses, but where does the other go?"

For a moment Burns hesitated; then he replied, "I don't guess it'll hurt none to tell you. That left-hand trail goes to the Velarde place, and there's another fork a ways along that ends up at the spread that belongs to the Hinojosas."

"How far is it to the Rancho Velarde?" Jessie asked.

"From here, it's close to twelve miles. And the Hinojosa place is a mite further. But if you hadn't got off on the wrong fork of that road last night, you'd a got to the Velarde main house after you'd gone maybe six miles."

After they'd gone a bit further, they could hear the high-pitched shriek of the sawmill, and as they made the final turn in the path that wound between the tree stumps and the settlement, they saw that the sawmill was little more than a high roof with one side wall and one end wall completed. The side facing the lake was open to make it easier to haul the logs from the millpond, and the end where the saw stood had also been left unfinished to allow the finished boards to be hauled away.

When the men in the mill saw the trio approaching, the saw's penetrating shrilling stopped and they left the building's cover. The men working the millpond put their peaveys aside and started toward them as well. With the silencing of the saw, the doors of several of the cabins opened and women appeared in them.

"Who in hell's them two, Mike?" one of the sawmill workers called as he approached the new arrivals.

"They're some folks from outside, Boyd," Burns replied. "Said they was looking for the Velarde place and taken the wrong turn at the fork the other side of the ridge. They was bedded down in that arroyo just over the valley rim."

"So you brought 'em in for us to look over." The man, whose name was Tim Boyd, nodded approvingly.

"Maybe it'd be more like it to say they brought me in," Burns said sheepishly. "I guess you can see who's got my rifle."

Boyd glanced at the rifle in Ki's hands and turned back to Burns. He asked, "How in hell did they get your rifle?"

"I ain't right sure yet, but they made it look real easy. Oh, they're real fighters, Boyd, take my word for it."

"Maybe you'd better let us speak for ourselves," Jessie broke in.

"Go ahead, lady. We're listening," Boyd told her.

"To begin with, the only member of the Velarde family I know is Teresa Velarde. She and I were schoolmates back east several years ago," Jessie explained. "She invited me to visit her, and that's what I came here to do."

"What about that Indian with you?" Boyd asked.

Ki spoke for himself. "I am not an Indian, Mr. Boyd. My name is Ki, I am of Japanese ancestry, and I am Miss Starbuck's assistant. She has a ranch in Texas and other businesses, and I help her to look after them."

65

"That's the same thing he told me," Mike Burns broke in. "I didn't believe it at first, but I'm beginning to now."

Jessie took up her interrupted explanation. "Mr. Burns has told you how he found us. He threatened us with his rifle, and neither Ki nor I likes to be threatened, so we disarmed him. He asked us to come here with him and listen to your explanation of his lawless conduct, and we agreed."

"If they're quick-draw artists like Mike says," one of the sawmill workers broke in, "old Velarde might've brought 'em up here to help him put us off his land."

"Now, let's just everybody wait a minute while I get all this sorted out," Boyd said quickly. He turned back to face Jessie and Ki, and asked, "You claim you don't know about the trouble we got here?"

Jessie shook her head. "The first time we knew there was any trouble was when Mr. Burns told us. But we still don't know what it's all about. Suppose you tell us, Mr. Boyd."

"It goes back quite a spell," Boyd said. "Us and our womenfolks come out here when the Reconstruction begun. We wasn't of a mind to let the damn Yankees boss us around. Now, back home in Georgia, on the Yellow River, I had me the purtiest sawmill you ever seen. It was burnt out during the War, and most of the boys that was working for me was burnt out, too. So, just as soon as we could scrape and save a little bit, we picked up and come to New Mexico Territory to start fresh."

Boyd paused for breath, and Jessie broke in, "It looks like you've succeeded quite well, Mr. Boyd. I've learned a little bit about lumbering and logging, and your mill looks very good."

"Oh, it'll pass muster," Boyd replied. He tried to speak casually, but pride showed in his voice. Then his face grew sober, and he added, "But it looks like we're going to lose it."

"How's that?"

"Well, we bought our land offen old Don Esteban Velarde," Boyd explained. "Only, it seems like it wasn't rightly his to sell. Some kind of mortgage that he never did tell us about. He kept promising to give us the deed, but he never did deliver it. Now he's saying he can't give us a deed to land we've done paid for, and he might have to give the land back to the fellow that he bought it from way back before we ever showed up."

"Who would that be?" Jessie asked.

"Another one of his own kind, the old aristocrats. There's a word they use for 'em up here in the Rio Arriba, Miss Starbuck. *Ricos,* they're called."

"If I remember, *rico* means 'rich,'" Jessie said.

"That's right," Boyd said, nodding. "The other one's name is Don Antonio Hinojosa."

"And Don Antonio won't acknowledge your purchase from Don Esteban?" Jessie asked.

"Not so's you'd notice."

"Them old *ricos* is all alike," one of the men growled. "They want it all for theirselves, nothing for folks like us."

"Have you talked to Don Antonio?" Jessie asked.

Boyd shook his head. "Me and a couple of the boys went to see him. He wouldn't give an inch. Says if Don Esteban don't pay him, he's got somebody waiting to buy our land and the sawmill and all the houses we built on it."

While they'd been talking, men and women from the cabins had been trickling down singly and in pairs to join the men from the mill. So far they'd been content to listen, but now one of the women spoke.

"It's taken my man and me six years of squeezin' and

67

scrapin' to git the money we needed to come out here," she said. "He's ready to fight iffen they try to take what little bit we got away from us."

A murmur of approval swept through the little group. Burns said, "Both of them old *ricos* is just the same. Now that somebody's come along to buy us out, old Hinojosa sees he's got a chance to make double his money by selling, and old Velarde sees a chance to have somebody else pay off what Hinojosa claims he still owes."

"They ain't got much use for one another, them two old men," Boyd added. "But we figure they'd forget about that and gang up on us if they got a chance to."

"Maybe you should try talking to them again," Ki suggested.

"We've tried to, but they won't let us get close to their houses, neither one of 'em. That's why we got to thinking they might be bringing in some hired guns, to run us off so they can set down and work out a fresh deal between theirselves."

"And you thought we were coming here for that?" Jessie asked.

"We don't know what to think, Miss Starbuck," Boyd told her. "We're just setting here, waiting, and you know there ain't nothing worse than that."

"This man you said Don Antonio Hinojosa has waiting to buy your land, do you know anything about him?" Jessie asked.

"Only that he's from back east someplace," Burns volunteered. "His name's Creighton. He stopped here, and after he nosed around and asked a lot of questions, he offered to buy us out lock, stock, and barrel. We didn't like his looks, and when we talked among ourselves, it didn't take us long to agree we wasn't selling. We told him we didn't want to make no deal with him, and he rode off."

"And you haven't seen him since?" Jessie asked.

"One other time. He come here with old Hinojosa, and the old man told us that Don Velarde didn't have no right to sell us this land. Hinojosa said it belonged to his family, and he was going to sell it to Creighton."

Jessie shook her head. "I can understand why all of you are nervous and keyed up," she said, "but do you believe now that Ki and I don't have any part in what's happening? It's exactly as I said from the beginning: the only reason I'm here is to visit my school friend."

"Oh, I figured that out pretty quick after we begun talking," Boyd replied. "And I don't see any reason why a lady like you—one that's friendly with the Velarde family— why you'd pay any mind to our troubles. But maybe now that you know what's going on, you might be able to give us some help."

"I don't know what I could do," she said.

"Could you just talk to old Don Esteban?" Boyd asked. "All he'd have to do is pay off what he owes Hinojosa, and that'd settle this whole mess."

Jessie thought for a moment, then nodded. "All right, Mr. Boyd. When I've met Don Esteban, I'll try to talk to him and tell him your situation. But I can't promise you that I'll be able to persuade him to do anything."

"Well, I sure hope you can get him to do something about it, Miss Starbuck," Boyd said, "because I'm telling you the truth. All of us has fought for what we had back home in Georgia, and wound up losing. And we might wind up losing again. But this land we're standing on is all that we got in the world, and I promise you, we'll fight to keep it!"

Chapter 7

"Fighting doesn't always settle things," Jessie said. "I'll be glad to talk to Don Esteban and tell him what you've told me, but I can't promise he'll do anything."

"We'll be grateful for your help, whatever you try to do, Miss Starbuck," Burns said. "It's real nice of you to offer, after the way I butted in on your camp, but I reckon now you can see why I did."

"Of course," Jessie said. "And if you're satisfied now that we didn't come up here to do you any harm, we'd better get on our way."

"You can't start traveling on an empty stomach!" he protested. "Wait just a minute." Rising on tiptoe, Burns looked out over the group of Big Piney people who'd come to see what was happening. He called, "Samantha! You got enough venison left from that deer I brought in last week to feed Miss Starbuck and Ki, ain't you?"

From the back of the group, a tall round-cheeked woman replied, "It's in the stew kittle now, Mike. Bring them over to the cabin when you're done talking, and I'll fill 'em up."

As they sat around a home-carpentered table in the tiny crowded cabin, eating tasty venison stew, Jessie said, "I'm curious about that man you mentioned who offered to buy your sawmill before this trouble with Don Antonio started. I think you said his name was Creighton."

"That's right. I don't know as I can tell you much about him, except he was dead set on buying us out."

"Was he from the territory here?" Jessie asked.

Burns shook his head, swallowed the piece of meat he was chewing, and replied, "No. Someplace back east. Talked like one of them Easterners, too, sorta la-di-da."

"This mill's so far from a railroad. From what I've seen of the roads in this Rio Arriba country, it occurs to me that you must have trouble getting your lumber to market."

"Oh, it ain't all that bad," Burns said. "Mostly, what we sell is rough-cut boards for mine shoring and farm buildings. Just about all of it goes to the mines in Colorado, and it ain't too bad a haul to the D&RG and Santa Fe, even over the kind of roads we got."

"Did Creighton plan to keep on selling to the mines that've been buying from you regularly?" Jessie asked.

"If he did, he didn't talk about it. He did tell us he had a lot of customers all lined up to buy from him. I guess that's why he was so all-fired anxious. He said timbering's real costly up there in Colorado."

"It would be, of course," Ki agreed. "Most of the timber in Colorado is on federal land, and the government's pretty stingy about issuing cutting permits, from what I've heard."

"That's what Creighton said, too," Burns told them. "He got right mad when we refused his offer; he was so sure we was going to sell out to him."

"How'd he come to that idea?"

"I ain't sure, Miss Starbuck. You see, all of us is in this together. Share and share alike was how we begun, and

71

that's how we've stayed. But now that things has settled down back home, some of the womenfolks have a mind to go back. I guess they would, if they had the money. But like I said, we talked it over and decided not to sell."

"With a good market for timber so close by, I can see why Creighton would be upset to see his deal fall through," Jessie said thoughtfully.

"He wasn't just upset," Burns told her. "He was madder'n a wet hen. Cussed and carried on and wound up telling us he was going to have this place one way or another. Then later, we found out he'd gone to Hinojosa and worked him up a when-and-if deal. He'd get the timber and mill when and if we was pushed off. And that didn't set so well with us, I'll tell you."

"I see," Jessie said thoughtfully. She pushed her plate away and turned to Samantha Burns. "Your stew really hit the spot, Mrs. Burns. Thank you for feeding us."

"I couldn't say it better than Jessie did," Ki chimed in. "I didn't know how hungry I was until I began eating."

"You're right welcome, I'm sure," Mrs. Burns replied. "And if you come back this way any time, be sure to look in. There's most always a pot of deer meat on the hob."

Jessie and Ki stood up, and Burns followed their example. He said, "Now, that path up to the Velarde place is sorta rough, but you ain't got too far to go. And there's only the one fork in it. You keep to your left when you get to it. The other fork takes you to the Hinojosa place."

Jessie and Ki set out, riding through a forest of stumps across the land bordering the lake. Looking across the sparkling blue water, they could see that on the opposite shore the big pines had also been cut. As they rode upslope on their way out of the valley, they entered another area of virgin forest. Here the pine trees stood thick and grew tall, the trail winding between the towering trunks. Even when they reached the valley's rim, the pine stands stretched out ahead of them.

"I can see why somebody would want this land, Ki," Jessie remarked. "It's one of the best areas for lumbering that we've seen since we left Santa Fe."

"It sure is," Ki agreed. "A downhill haul all the way to the lake, and a stream to run the sawmill. I can't say I blame this fellow Creighton for wanting it."

"I can't understand why Teresa's grandfather would want to sell it," Jessie said. "It seems to me the Velardes could have been producing lumber from it instead of just letting it stay idle and unproductive."

"I have an idea about that," Ki told her. "My hunch is that Spanish aristocrats of the old school are like the nobility of my own country. They look on some occupations as being beneath their dignity even to notice."

"You may be right," she answered. "I've noticed that aristocrats the world over think in pretty uniform terms, regardless of nationality, and I suppose the Spanish noble families would look at things pretty much the same way."

As they rode on through the cloudless morning, the upward slope of the ground grew less pronounced and the huge pines gave way abruptly to the same kind of low-growing pinyon trees that they'd seen the evening before. They were just leaving the last of the pine forest when a large painted board nailed to one of the towering trees beside the trail caught their eyes. As they drew closer, Jessie and Ki saw that the board was a sign of some kind. They reached it and pulled up their mounts.

In bold black letters the sign proclaimed: *"FRONTERA DE LA MERCED DE TIERRA ROJA. Patentado y confirmado en el año 1854 por la Corte Suprema de los Estados*

Unidos y por el Agrimensor General del Territorio de Neuvo Mexico. Declara! Que calquier persona quebrante en dicho merced, se castigado bajo los leyes de dicha territorio por propietario. ESTEBAN VELARDE."

"My Spanish isn't up to translating it," Ki said.

"Neither is mine," Jessie admitted. "All I can tell is that it's got something to do with the Velardes because it has Don Esteban's name on it."

"That must be one of the signs the people at Big Piney were talking about," Ki said. "It seems an odd place for it, though, if the Velardes claim the land beyond it down to the lake."

"My guess is that it's posted here because of the trail," Jessie told him. "I imagine there are other signs at the actual boundary lines."

Before Ki could reply, they heard hoofbeats approaching on the winding trail ahead. They fell silent, waiting, and in a few moments the rider appeared. He was a young man, not much past thirty, Spanish by his looks and of the Rio Arriba gentry by his clothing and saddle gear.

He wore the flat-crowned, wide-brimmed hat common to the few *vaqueros* Jessie and Ki had seen in Santa Fe and on their trip north, an embroidered waist-length *charro* jacket, and flared trousers that almost covered highly polished boots. He did not wear a pistol belt, but a rifle rested in its scabbard at the back of his silver-trimmed saddle. His horse was groomed until its coal-black coat shone like enamel.

When the rider saw Jessie and Ki he slowed his horse to a walk and reined in when he reached them. He doffed his hat to Jessie, and favored Ki with a half nod. When he spoke, his English was as flawless as Jessie's; only his intonation gave a hint that it was a second language.

"Good morning," he said. He looked from Jessie and Ki

to the sign, and grimaced. "With your permission, señorita. I am Felipe Hinojosa y Aragon."

"My name's Jessie Starbuck," Jessie told him. "And this is Ki. We're on our way to visit one of my old friends, Teresa Velarde."

Except for a flicker at the corners of his lips, the new arrival did not react. He said, "You'll forgive me for making a personal observation, Miss Starbuck, but you don't strike me as being one of the colonists from Big Piney."

"I'm not," Jessie replied. "My home is in Texas."

"I see." Felipe nodded. "May I ask if you started up here from Santa Fe?"

"I don't see the point of your question," Jessie said somewhat tartly. "But yes, we did."

"You are not on the most direct road, then," the young man observed. "And you are not on Velarde land. This is Hinojosa property, Miss Starbuck." When Jessie's eyes darted to the sign, he went on, "I see that Don Esteban has been busy again. I had heard of these signs, and came looking for them to remove them. You have read it, I'm sure?"

"Not exactly," Ki said. "Neither Jessie nor I know Spanish that well."

"Then I will read it for you in English," Felipe replied. He turned his eyes toward the sign and went on, "The Grant of Tierra Roja. Patented and confirmed in the year 1854 by the Supreme Court of the United States and the Surveyor General of New Mexico Territory. Notice! Anyone trespassing on this grant will be punished by the laws of the territory and by the owner, Esteban Velarde."

"But you just said this land doesn't belong to the Velardes, but to the Hinojosas, your family," Jessie said.

"I spoke truly, Miss Starbuck," Felipe replied. "The land

was purchased from my family by Don Esteban Velarde, but he has never paid for it, and we have now reclaimed it."

"Then the sign doesn't mean anything?" she asked.

"It does not!" Felipe said, anger creeping into his tone. "As I mentioned, I have heard of these notices and came to take them down. You will permit me."

Reining his horse over to the tree, he drew the rifle from its scabbard and with its steel-ended butt pounded at the sign until the board splintered in several places. He tossed the shards to the ground and shrugged, then turned back to Jessie and Ki.

"So much for the Velarde lies," he said scornfully. When neither of them answered, Felipe went on, "This trail forks a short distance ahead, Miss Starbuck. The left-hand branch will take you to your destination. Now, if you will excuse me, I must go on about my business."

Jessie and Ki sat watching his back as Felipe Hinojosa rode down the winding trail and disappeared.

"Arrogant, isn't he?" Ki commented to Jessie.

"He certainly is," she replied. "It'll be interesting to see what Don Esteban does when we tell him how his sign was treated."

"I'll be even more interested in finding out the whole story that lies behind all this," Ki said as they started up the trail again. "There's a lot more than appears on the surface; I'm sure of that."

"Yes, I sensed that, too," Jessie agreed. They rode on in silence for a few minutes, and then she said, "Ki, maybe I'm looking for something that doesn't even exist, but isn't there a familiar pattern to what the people at Big Piney told us about the problems they've been having?"

"I don't believe you're seeing ghosts, Jessie," Ki said.

"I have that same feeling myself."

"Mining in Colorado, timber in New Mexico," Jessie went on thoughtfully. "They're both natural resources, the kind of things the cartel's most interested in. And from the little we've heard about this mysterious Creighton, he'd fit into the cartel pattern of operations, too."

"Jessie," Ki said, after they'd ridden silently again for a short distance, "wasn't this trip supposed to be a vacation?"

"Of course. And I'm not looking for trouble, Ki. But if our suspicions are correct and trouble starts, I don't intend to run away from it."

Ki nodded and said nothing more. A short distance ahead, they could see where the trail forked, and they bore left as they were told. The character of the land they were crossing changed once more as they passed out of the narrow strip of piñon growth and rode onto grassland. It had little resemblance to the range they were accustomed to riding on the Circle Star, however. Instead of prairie rolling endlessly from horizon to horizon, this range was broken by cuts and valleys and rock outcrops. The grass was not high and waving, but short, ground-hugging growth.

Looking at the terrain through rancher's eyes, Jessie said, "Sheep country, Ki."

"It's certainly not cattle range," he agreed. "Too broken up. But controlled flocks of sheep, yes, as long as there are shepherds to watch over them."

Within another mile or two, the angular rooflines of buildings came into view. The clear air made distances deceptive, but Jessie judged that the buildings were still three or four miles away. They looked much closer, though, and the high jagged mountains that towered beyond them on the horizon seemed little more than a stone's throw from the settlement.

77

"I think we're finally getting there, Ki," she said. "That can't be anything but the Velarde ranch."

"It looks more like a small town than a ranch," Ki replied. "But I suppose that's what it is, all right."

As they drew closer, the buildings took shape. There were more than two dozen of them, chunky earth-hugging houses and long structures that looked like barns and stables. All of them were dominated by the big house that stood a little apart, surrounded by a low wall. Like the smaller buildings, the three-story mansion was made of adobe bricks, a mixture of the native soil and straw and water, and the walls plastered over with a mortar made also from adobe.

None of the houses—not even the big one—was painted, though the window casings and door frames of most of the dwellings were outlined in a blue that seemed to tie them together with the earth and sky. Rising from the brown soil, the buildings looked as much a part of the landscape as did the flanks of the jagged mountains that rose beyond them.

"I knew Teresa's family was well-off," Jessie told Ki as they drew closer to the houses and could see the extent of the settlement. "I didn't expect to see all this, though. The Circle Star's a good-sized spread, but we get along with a bunkhouse and dining room and a stable in addition to the main house. You were right a minute ago. That's a town ahead."

"It's a good-sized establishment," Ki agreed. "But when you think how isolated it is, and that they must be running sheep instead of cattle, it stands to reason that it'd have to be pretty well self-sustaining."

"I'm sure it is," Jessie said. "It's certainly big enough to be."

They rode on toward the clustered buildings. Jessie could tell almost to the instant when they were noticed approaching. A man ran from the village (she could not keep from thinking of the twenty or so small dwellings as a village) to the large house, and in a few moments the entire area burst into activity. They could see men running to the stables and corrals, and women starting for the big house.

Before Jessie and Ki had covered half the distance to the ranch, the men were leading saddled horses through a gate in the wall surrounding the big house. Within a few more minutes a small procession—four men riding behind a man and a woman—emerged from the arched gate that stood in the center of the front wall and started out to meet them.

"Even if it's too far to see her clearly, I'm sure that's Teresa on the white horse in front of the other's," Jessie exclaimed as the gap between her and the greeting party narrowed. "And I suppose the man riding by her on the big roan must be her grandfather."

"They're certainly doing things in great style," Ki said. "I think the Spanish must be as fond of ceremony as my own people are."

A long time seemed to pass as the two parties came together. When a hundred yards still separated them, the girl on the white horse spurred her mount. She left her companions and galloped toward the new arrivals.

"Jessie!" the girl called loudly, her excited shout carrying over the thudding of her horse's hoofbeats.

Almost at the same moment, Jessie raised her voice and cried, "Teresa!"

They came together and reined their horses close. Leaning from their saddles, the two women embraced. Then they broke into excited chattering, both of them talking at the same time.

Even as close as he was, Ki could catch only an occasional word. He timed his approach to bring him to the two women at the same time Teresa's party reached the spot, and he waited until the two women noticed that they were no longer alone.

Jessie was the first to break her conversation with her old school friend. She said, "I've mentioned Ki in my letters to you, Teresa. Ki, I'm sure you and Teresa don't need any introduction."

Ki bowed without dismounting. "Miss Velarde," he said. "I am honored to meet you."

"Please," she replied. "You must call me by my first name, just as Jessie does." Belatedly, she realized that the rest of her escorting party had reined in and was waiting. She went on, "Jessie, and you too, Ki. Come and meet my grandfather."

Jessie and Ki followed Teresa as she walked her white steed toward the men. Jessie took stock of Teresa's grandfather without appearing to do so. The old *hacendado* sat his mount with the casually erect ease of a skilled horseman, though from his thin and wrinkled face Jessie judged him to be in his seventies.

Don Esteban Velarde wore a full white moustache, its tips curled and tightly waxed, and long sideburns that had been carefully shaved into crescents that curved below his hatbrim almost to the tips of his moustache. His high-bridged nose was thin and resembled the beak of a hawk. Below bristling white eyebrows, his sunken black eyes glistened with an interest that belied his age.

His gold-embroidered *charro* jacket worn over a creamy silk shirt hinted at a sparse but still-muscular body. The shirt was caught up with a thin black bow tie that confined the loose wrinkles sagging from chin to throat. His trousers matched the shirt, and were belted at the waist with a wide sash of deep maroon.

Though Don Esteban raised his bristling white eyebrows as the three walked their horses toward him, he said nothing and let Teresa speak first.

"Abuelito," she said. "You need no introduction to Jessie. I've spoken of her so much. And this is her companion, Ki."

Don Esteban acknowledged Jessie with a bow, and inclined his head in Ki's general direction. Then he faced Jessie and said, "I am pleased that you have at last accepted Teresa's invitation to visit her here at Tierra Roja, Miss Starbuck. My house is yours. You honor us with your presence."

Chapter 8

"Thank you, Don Esteban," Jessie replied to the stately gentleman's welcome. "Your house looks very beautiful. I'm sure we'll enjoy our visit."

Before her grandfather could speak, Teresa broke in, "And I hope you've come to stay a long time, Jessie! We've got so much to catch up on! I've been counting the days until you got here."

"She has indeed, Miss Starbuck," Don Esteban said. "Each morning at breakfast Teresa has told me of something new that she must talk with you about." A frown growing on his face, he went on, "But we looked for you to get here sooner. Was your journey delayed for some reason?"

"Nothing important," Jessie replied. "We'd have been here yesterday, but we turned off the road at the wrong place and didn't realize we'd made a mistake until sundown. Then we decided to stop rather than trying to travel in the dark."

"You were not discommoded, I trust?" he asked.

"No. Or very little. We were frightened when someone fired a few shots at our camp during the night, but whoever it was didn't bother us."

"Cabalgadores de la noche!" Teresa exclaimed. *"Sali-den otra vez, abuelito!"* Seeing a frown flit over Jessie's face, she added quickly, "There are small groups of lawless men here on the Tierra Roja now and then, Jessie. We do not know who they are or where they come from. We call them night riders."

"Silencio, Teresa!" Don Esteban said sharply. He turned to Jessie and went on, "It is nothing, Miss Starbuck. A young girl's excitement." Turning to Teresa, he said quickly, *"Mas tarde hablamos de esto."*

Teresa nodded and said meekly, *"Si, abuelito."*

If his exchange with Teresa had upset Don Esteban, his voice did not reflect it when he turned back to Jessie and said, "We waste time, Miss Starbuck. Let us ride to the house, where we can sit in comfort while we wait for our meal."

Without waiting for Jessie to reply, the old man wheeled his horse and led the way toward the walled house. The men of the escort waited until their master and his guests had started, and then fell in behind them. The group rode in silence through the thick wooden gates that enclosed the hacienda, and followed Don Esteban to the front door.

It was a double door, as wide as the gate and made from boards just as thick. The portals swung open as though of their own accord as Don Esteban dismounted and led the way inside. The hallway seemed dim to Jessie as she and Teresa followed Don Esteban inside. Ki walked behind them, and bringing up the rear were two men from the escort, carrying the saddlebags they'd taken from the newcomers' horses.

Without looking back, Don Esteban flicked a hand as they made their way down the hall, and the men deposited the saddlebags on the floor and went back outside. The others followed Don Esteban into a room that opened off the hall, a long narrow room with high-set windows that were little more than slits, but that made the room brighter than the corridor.

"We will eat soon," the old man said, indicating chairs and a divan with a gesture. "But while we wait, Miss Starbuck, I will take the opportunity to apologize to you for the rude reception you received last night and explain to you a few things about this Rio Arriba country."

"You don't need to apologize for last night, Don Esteban," Jessie said as she settled onto the leather-upholstered divan beside Teresa. "I certainly don't hold you responsible for what some roving band of outlaws must've done."

"Perhaps *explain* would be a better word," the old man said, sitting down in an ornately carved high-backed chair near the divan. As you are here for what Teresa and I hope will be a long visit, you must understand the Rio Arriba."

"I don't need to understand it to know that I like it very much," Jessie replied. "It's beautiful country. But I'll admit that I'm still curious about the shooting last night."

"I'm sure that Teresa's remarks about the *cabalgadores*, the night riders, must have puzzled you," Don Esteban went on. "It is a thing which we accept as part of our lives, you see. This land of ours is far from Santa Fe, and during the years since we have settled here, we have learned to expect little from the central government. We ranchers enforce our own laws and ask of the authorities in Santa Fe only to be left alone."

"And the night riders?" Jessie asked when he paused.

"Are lawless men, most of them fugitives from crimes, who have come to use our forested lands as a hiding place," the old man explained. "Since the attack on your camp last night took place on Velarde land, I will send my men to track down those who disturbed you. They will be punished, Miss Starbuck."

"A sort of sheriff's posse, with you and the other ranch owners acting in place of an elected sheriff?" Ki suggested.

Don Esteban was obviously not accustomed to being questioned by anyone he considered to be a servant. He looked at Ki for a moment, a frown forming on his face, then from the corner of his eye saw Jessie watching expectantly. His voice stern, he said, "It is our duty as *hacendados* to maintain order on our land. This is the way things have always been here in the Rio Arriba. We do not expect others to do what we can do ourselves."

Jessie broke in quickly to ask, "Don't you have any elected officials here in the Rio Arriba, then?"

Don Esteban frowned as he replied, "Of course not. Why do we need them? We *hacendados* have always protected what is ours, and we will continue to do so."

Before Jessie could reply, a man who looked almost as old as Don Esteban came in. His white cotton trousers were evidence of his status as a servant, but his air of authority and the black jacket he wore indicated that he was a superior sort of servant. He bowed to Don Esteban and announced, *"La merienda aguardase, patrón."*

Don Esteban acknowledged the message with a nod. He stood up, saying, "Let us refresh ourselves, then. I am sure Miss Starbuck must be hungry, Teresa." He stepped aside to let Teresa and Jessie precede him to the door, then moved in front of Ki as he followed the women from the room.

Ki made no protest. He was used to having strangers take him for Jessie's servant, and their mistakes no longer bothered him. He followed Don Esteban, but at the door the man who'd announced luncheon put a hand on his arm and held him back.

"Please, señor," he said in a low voice. "Come with me, if you will. We will eat together, and while we eat we can talk of things that you must understand."

Ki hid his surprise, but nodded agreement. He followed the man down the corridor and caught his signal to wait while he went with Teresa, Jessie, and Don Esteban into a room a few steps down the hall. Ki could not resist peering into the room they'd entered, and he saw the man who'd detained him seating the trio at a table set for three. Then women came up the hall carrying dishes and platters, and Ki stepped aside. After a few moments, the man came out and extended his hand.

"I am Bartolome," he said in excellent English. "You must forgive me, señor Ki, but Teresa asked me to do what I did to avoid unpleasantness before the meal."

"Don Esteban didn't want me at the table?" Ki guessed.

"That is right. But if you don't mind eating with me—"

"I don't mind at all," Ki broke in. "It's a mistake I've gotten used to, and it doesn't bother me any longer."

As they walked down the hall, Bartolome explained. "Don Esteban is of a mind with the old *patrones,* such as his father. He was not always as he is now, you must understand. When we were boys together, we were like brothers. Then when my father—he was *mayordomo* to the Velarde family before me—when he died and I became *mayordomo,* it was as though a wall had been built between us. But I do not mind. Serving the Velardes is as much a part of my life as being served is a part of theirs."

"I can understand that quite well," Ki replied.

Ki followed Bartolome into a small room where a table set for two was waiting. He didn't bother to explain that the customs of his Japanese mother's family had been as inflexible as those followed by descendants of the grandees of old Spain. Bartolome motioned him to a chair, and they sat down.

"Teresa understands your position with Miss Starbuck from the letters they have exchanged," the *mayordomo* began. "She knew her grandfather would not, and together we worked out this arrangement to avoid disputes between her and Don Esteban."

"Then Teresa is a very smart girl," Ki said, watching Bartolome fill their plates with a chicken stew that steamed with a flavorful aroma as he ladled it out of a deep tureen.

"She would not hurt her grandfather. She loves him very much, and the two of them are the last of the family," Bartolome went on. "Between us, we arranged to have these private meals, and when you and Miss Starbuck need to talk privately, Teresa or I will arrange that, too."

"You seem to have thought of everything," Ki said.

"We tried," Bartolome answered. "Now, while we enjoy our meal, you and I must discuss the arrangements we've made to keep unpleasant accidents from marring your visit."

In the dining room, Jessie had interpreted Teresa's anxious looks and nods as a signal that she need not worry about Ki. Though Jessie did not approve of their separation, or of Don Esteban's arbitrary action, she'd gathered enough from the confidences she and Teresa had exchanged as schoolmates to realize that the Velarde ranch was so deeply rooted in old traditions and customs that trying to alter them was virtually impossible. She pacified Teresa's visible worry with a nod of understanding, and let the meal proceed.

Don Esteban set an example of silence by eating hungrily and saying virtually nothing until his plate was cleared. Only after the women serving them had removed the dinner plates, refilled their coffee cups, and brought a dessert of light cream whipped with a strong dash of vanilla did the old man begin to talk.

"I have not forgotten your unfortunate experience on your way to my rancho, Miss Starbuck. My men will be out looking for the night riders before sundown."

"Do you think they will be able to find them?" she asked.

With an expressive shrug, the old *hacendado* said, *"Quién sabe?* But they are skilled trackers. They will keep looking until they are successful or have found that the scoundrels have left the Tierra Roja."

Then he changed the subject abruptly and began asking Jessie her impressions of Santa Fe and of the lands she'd seen on the trip to the Rio Arriba. Jessie replied patiently for a while, and then began asking questions to satisfy her own curiosity.

"Please explain something to me," she said. "You call this the Rancho Velarde, but you've also mentioned the Tierra Roja. Is that another ranch on your property?"

"No, no," the old man answered. "The royal land grant made to my family so many years ago was called the Tierra Roja because most of it is on an area where the earth is quite red. Even before we received the grant, the Indians called this part of the Rio Arriba 'the land of red earth.'"

"There were Indians here?" Jessie asked. "Ki and I didn't see any on our trip."

"There are none now," he replied. "And they were always few in number. They had abandoned the few old pueblos northwest of Taos long before our people came from Spain. The nomadic tribes hunted over the land, but even then it held little game to draw them in large numbers."

"Then your family and the others who came with them were really the first settlers," Jessie said thoughtfully.

"We were, indeed. And except for the royal land grants, this land would still be deserted."

"I understand now why the king of Spain was so generous," Jessie told him. "He made those grants large to be sure the land would be settled by his own people."

"But your people upset his plans," Don Esteban replied. "It is far in the past now, and old bitterness is forgotten."

Jessie decided the time had come to ask the question she'd been leading up to. "I know that we on the Circle Star are far from our neighbors, but you must be even further if your neighbors also received large grants."

"Oh, the Tierra Roja is not the largest of the royal grants made in the Rio Arriba, Miss Starbuck," Don Esteban replied. "But neither is it the smallest."

"I'm afraid I don't know enough about the Rio Arriba country to be a good judge," she said. "Do you mind telling me how large it is, Don Esteban?"

"Of course not. The grant consisted of about a million hectares."

Jessie struggled for a moment with the mental arithmetic required to convert hectares to acres, then looked at him with astonishment. "But that's more than a quarter-million acres!" she exclaimed.

"Yes, but you have a large ranch in Texas, Miss Starbuck. Surely the size of the Tierra Roja grant does not surprise you."

"But it does. How do you keep track of such a vast spread?"

Don Esteban countered with a question of his own. "How do you keep track of your own ranch?"

"Why, with a dozen hard-riding hands and a good foreman."

"Then there is only a difference of size between your method and mine." Don Esteban shrugged. "I have twenty-four families, and half as many more men without families, living on the Tierra Roja. Many of them were born here and look on the Rancho Velarde as their home, which it is."

"That explains something that's been puzzling me, then," Jessie said. "Ki and I saw no cattle on our way here, and I wondered where your herds were. But I suppose you have them on land that we didn't pass through."

"To be sure. Most of the cattle are on the northern ranges now. The sheep are to the west, on land unsuited for cattle."

Teresa had been growing increasingly restless while her grandfather and Jessie were talking. She broke in now to say, "Jessie came to visit me, *abuelito,* but we've barely had time to say hello. I'm going to take her to my room now for our *siesta,* so we can talk of things that would not interest you."

"It was my thought that you would do this, my dear," the old man said with a smile. "That is why I have not hesitated to talk with her so much of the time during our meal. Go now, you two. I must attend to a few details before I enjoy my own *siesta.*"

Jessie discovered that what Teresa had referred to as her "room" was actually a series of connected rooms that took up one corner of the big hacienda's second floor. In addition to Teresa's corner bedroom there was a guest bedroom, and each had its own cozy sitting room and bath.

"These were the rooms my parents occupied before they died," Teresa explained. "When I was old enough, Grandfather told me that he had reserved them for me and my future husband."

"Before you say anything else, please tell me what happened to Ki, and why he didn't come into the dining room with us," Jessie said.

"Of course. I couldn't say anything while Grandfather was with us," Teresa explained. "He is of the stern old

90

school and thinks it's beneath his dignity to eat with a servant."

"Ki isn't a servant," Jessie broke in quickly. "He was my father's helper and his friend. That's what he is to me."

"I find him very interesting," Teresa said. "He looks like he could be of the Pueblo people, even though I know better."

"Ki's father was American, his mother Japanese," Jessie explained, and went on to tell Teresa how Ki had been hired by Alex Starbuck and had remained with her after Alex's murder.

"It seems so long ago," Teresa sighed.

"Yes. But you still haven't explained how and why Ki just dropped out of sight on the way to the dining room."

"I arranged with Bartolome to have his meals in a small dining room with Ki," Teresa explained. "I may have done wrong, Jessie, but I didn't want an argument with Grandfather to spoil your visit."

"I suppose I understand," Jessie said with a frown. "But I want to find out how Ki feels before I say anything more."

"You're not angry with me, are you?"

"Of course not! I know how you feel about your grandfather, Teresa, even if I can't understand how he feels about Ki. Where is Ki now, by the way?"

"Bartolome will bring him up here as soon as Grandfather's asleep. That won't be very long, so please be patient with me, Jessie, and not angry."

"Of course I'll be patient," Jessie said. "And I'm not what you'd call angry, just puzzled."

"It'll be settled soon," Teresa promised. "You know that if this were my house, I'd have acted differently."

"Of course. It seems to me you *should* have your own house by now, Teresa, and a husband and a child or two.

91

Is there a husband in sight?"

"Of course not!" Teresa told her. "Where in the Rio Arriba would I find one?"

"Surely you have neighbors," Jessie suggested.

Teresa said, "You've forgotten what I told you about the ranch when we were in school, Jessie. Our nearest neighbors on the east are fifteen miles away, and to the west almost thirty miles. The nearest town is Taos, which is even harder to reach than Santa Fe, even if Santa Fe is further away."

"I guess I had forgotten," Jessie replied. "But surely you have visitors?"

"Not often. You're the first guest to stay here in four months. Now do you understand why my letters are unhappy?"

"I suppose I didn't really realize how isolated you are," Jessie said. "But I remember you wrote me that you had a suitor at one time, soon after you'd graduated from Miss Booth's."

"I did. A young army officer from Fort Marcy. I met him in Santa Fe, and we—well, you wouldn't be interested after such a long time. But now..." Teresa shrugged.

"Just be patient," Jessie advised. "Someone will be along when the time is right."

"And that might not be until I'm a wrinkled old woman, the way things are now," Teresa replied. "But what about you, Jessie? Is Ki—"

"Just as I said a minute ago, Ki is to me exactly what he was to Alex, a good friend and loyal helper. Now, let's wait until he gets here before we talk any more about him. Tell me what you've been doing since we saw each other last."

"There isn't much to tell," Teresa sighed. "Nothing much happens here on the ranch. When—" She broke off as a

92

light tapping sounded on the door, and she went to open it. Ki and Bartolome stood in the hallway.

"Your idea was very good, señorita," the *mayordomo* said as he and Ki slipped into the room. "Ki understands your situation better than I had thought he might."

"Don't worry about me, Jessie," Ki said quickly. "Now that Bartolome has explained, I can sympathize with Teresa's problem. It is very much like the one my mother had, but it doesn't bother me a bit."

"As long as you're sure," Jessie said.

"I'm sure," Ki answered. "And I can't think of anything we need to talk about now, so I won't intrude on your reunion with Teresa. My room is on the third floor, but Bartolome will arrange for us to talk privately if we need to."

"It will be easy, señorita," Bartolome assured Jessie. "You will only need to whisper Ki's name to me, and I will see to it that you meet at once, in private."

"I suppose it's the best solution," Jessie agreed reluctantly. "All right, Ki. We'll let the arrangement stand, and Teresa and I will go on with our talk."

Chapter 9

"Thank you, Jessie," Teresa said after Ki and Bartolome had left.

"For what? I haven't done anything."

"Yes, you have. You've been as understanding as you always were with my little problems at school."

"Just guessing, I'd say those problems at school were small compared to the ones you're having now," Jessie said. "And we haven't seen each other for such a long time that I don't really know what they are. Maybe you'd better start by telling me what's happened to you since I left Miss Booth's."

"Yes. And let's sit the way we used to in our room there, Jessie. It'll seem like time has been standing still."

Jessie levered out of her boots and the two settled on the bed. They sat Indian style, ankles crossed, facing each other, one at the head, the other at the foot.

"Now I can feel like we've never been apart," Teresa said. She sat silently for a moment, then began, "When you left school, there wasn't anybody there I could talk to. Not the way we'd talked, anyhow. Oh, I was very lonely, Jessie."

"Surely things have been better since you came home."

"For a while, they were. But when I'd been back here for about a year after graduation, I met Lieutenant Andrews at a dance given by some of our Santa Fe friends. We fell in love almost instantly. It was such a wonderful feeling, Jessie! I was so happy!"

"Why didn't you marry him?" Jessie asked. "You wrote me that you intended to get married, then in your next letter you said you weren't, but you never did give me all the details."

"I was too sad and upset to write about it," Teresa confessed. "You see, Jessie, after Roger—Lieutenant Andrews—asked me to marry him, I had to get Grandfather's permission."

"Of course. I understand that." Jessie nodded.

"Grandfather was having some trouble with cattle buyers at that time," Teresa went on. "He had to spend more time than usual in the capital, and of course he always took me with him, so I could see Roger more than I'd have been able to usually. And when I arranged for them to meet after Roger asked me to marry him, Grandfather approved of our engagement."

"Which you hadn't expected him to do?"

"I was afraid he wouldn't. No Velarde woman had ever even thought of marrying anyone except our own kind before."

"And so you set a date for the wedding?"

Teresa shook her head. "No. Grandfather said it was his place to do that."

Jessie was sure she knew what was coming, but she said nothing, just nodded understandingly and waited for Teresa to continue.

"But I didn't mind, because Roger and I could be together

when I went with Grandfather to Santa Fe. And he understood why we had to wait. But we were so in love, Jessie! We needed one another! So Roger rented a little room where we could meet and be together."

"Don Esteban didn't know about that, I suppose."

"Of course not!" Teresa exclaimed. "I . . ." She hesitated and then went on, her voice quivering, "I didn't even mention it to my priest when I went to confession."

To give Teresa time to compose herself, Jessie said consolingly, "I might have made the same decision if I'd have been in your place."

"Grandfather delayed setting a date for our wedding," Teresa continued after a moment. "And—well, you can probably guess that I—I was—"

"You were pregnant," Jessie said bluntly.

Teresa nodded, her lips compressed. She swallowed hard and said, "Then Roger was killed leading his men in a skirmish with some hostile Indians."

"And what did you do, Teresa?" Jessie asked, her sympathy showing in her voice. "Tell Don Esteban?"

"No. There is an old woman, a *curandera*, who lives with her grandchildren here on the ranch." Teresa's voice trembled, and Jessie could see that she was fighting back tears. "I went to her and she mixed me a tea of herbs that took away the little baby I had growing inside me. Grandfather did not know about the baby. He thought I was only mourning for Roger."

"You've had some bad times," Jessie said gently. "Why didn't you write me, Teresa? If I'd known, I could've come here for a visit when you needed me, instead of waiting so long."

"I tried to write you," Teresa confessed. "But everything I put on paper came out wrong. Now that all seems to have happened a long time ago; it's as if it happened to somebody else, not to me. I just had to tell you, because——"

"Because I'm the only one you have to tell such things to," Jessie broke in.

"Yes. And telling you has made me feel better."

"I'm glad. But what about the future? Isn't there anybody on one of the other Rio Arriba ranches that you——"

"If there is, I haven't met him yet."

"Ki and I ran into one of your neighbors on our way here this morning. I haven't mentioned it because he was tearing down a sign that Don Esteban had posted warning trespassers off the Tierra Roja grant, and I wanted to talk to you about it before saying anything to your grandfather."

"That was wise, Jessie," Teresa said with a nod. "Please don't say anything about it. Grandfather would be terribly angry."

"I had an idea that he would be. But he's sure to find out, sooner or later."

"Better later than now, Jessie," Teresa said. "The man you met must have been either Diego or Felipe Hinojosa, one of Don Antonio's twin grandsons."

Jessie nodded. "It was Felipe. And I don't know that I'd care to meet him again. He was very arrogant and conceited."

"Now I'm sure it was Felipe." Teresa smiled. "Diego is not at all like his brother. He is thoughtful and courteous."

"But you don't think of him as a prospective husband?"

"No. There is not a good feeling between the Hinojosas and the Velardes, Jessie."

"So I gathered. Has it been that way a long time?"

"As long as I can remember," Teresa replied.

"What started the ill feeling?"

"I'm not really sure, Jessie. Something about the grant boundaries or some land that changed hands between us years ago. Grandfather has never explained it to me completely. He's of the old school. It's his belief that women shouldn't be involved in business affairs."

"But you'll own the Tierra Roja grant someday!" Jessie protested. "Even if you're married, the land will go to you."

"Of course. But I can't change Grandfather's beliefs. I've tried, but he just doesn't listen."

"Well, keep trying," Jessie said.

"Oh, I intend to." Teresa fought back a yawn, then went on, "Don't you think we'd better rest for a while now? I'll confess, I'm so used to my daily *siesta* that I'm getting a bit sleepy after all our talking."

When Jessie awoke from her nap the afternoon was half-gone, and when she looked into Teresa's room it was empty. She went downstairs and found Teresa sitting with Don Esteban in the parlor.

"I was just going up to wake you," Teresa said. "Grandfather thought you might like to look at the ranch."

"A short ride only," Don Esteban added. "A look at the corrals and stables, and a stroll through the *placita* where our people make their homes. I have already taken the liberty of telling Bartolome to have a horse saddled for you."

"Wouldn't it be just as easy to walk?" Jessie asked.

"Perhaps," the old man replied. "But it would set a bad example for our people. You see, Miss Starbuck, on the ranches of the Rio Arriba the *peones* all walk. For them to ride would be above their station in life."

"I don't suppose we'll be seeing any of your range cattle, then?" she asked.

Don Esteban smiled. "To reach our cattle range is a full day's ride. And our sheep pastureland is still further from the hacienda."

"I think you'll enjoy looking at our horses, Jessie," Teresa said. "You've told me about your palomino, Sun, and we have three fine palomino broodmares and a very good stallion."

Jessie did indeed enjoy watching the palominos cavorting in their own small corral, though privately she told herself that the stallion was nowhere near as fine as Sun. She was amazed at the size and number of barns and sheds and other auxiliary buildings on the ranch, until she realized that, unlike the warm climate she enjoyed year-round at the Circle Star, the winters in the high mountains were very cold indeed.

More than anything else, she was fascinated by the *placita*, the cluster of small adobe houses for the ranch workers. The *placita* was more extensive than she'd realized from the quick glimpse she'd had of it when she and Ki rode up. There were at least thirty houses, and in front of most of them small children played in the dusty red soil. At others, old men and women far past the age of hard work sat taking the sun. The *placita* was as large as some of the small villages she'd seen in her travels, and she wondered how the Rancho Velarde could require so many workers.

"Do all the people who live in these houses work for your ranch, Don Esteban?" she asked as they started back to the main house.

"Not all work now," he explained. "Those who are no longer able to work simply live out their lives in peace."

"Do you still pay them?"

"Only the men who work receive a regular wage," he said, "but we provide the old ones with food and clothing and wood for their fireplaces in winter. They served the Rancho Velarde well when they were young and strong, so it is my responsibility to give them a peaceful life now that they are no longer able to work."

"Just how many of the people on your ranch do you hire for regular work, then?" Jessie asked.

"You would have to ask Bartolome," the old man replied. "It is his job to look after such small details."

Jessie recognized evasion when she encountered it, and saw that she would get no real information from the old grandee. She asked no more questions, and after they returned to the house she excused herself from returning to the parlor and went up to her room. To her surprise, Ki was waiting for her.

"Bartolome had some things to look after," he told her. "I saw you coming back here and thought we might have a chance for a private talk."

"There's not really much to talk about, Ki. Don Esteban is very polite and proper, but he's also very closemouthed. I haven't had a chance to ask him about the people at Big Piney or the dispute he's having with the Hinojosa family over the land the sawmill's on."

"Bartolome's the same way," Ki said.

"I thought I'd be able to find out almost anything I wanted to know from Teresa. But it seems that here in the Rio Arriba, women aren't told much about what's really going on."

"We've been here such a short time that I don't suppose we could expect to find out a great deal," Ki pointed out.

"Maybe I'm too impatient," Jessie said. "Really, what I'm most interested in learning is if that man Creighton is trying to buy the sawmill and timberlands for the cartel. You're right, though. We haven't been here long enough to learn much."

"And we didn't come here on business, but for you to visit Teresa and to rest," Ki reminded her.

"That's what we'll do, then. If I can just get used to the idea that this is supposed to be a vacation."

"You will," Ki assured her. "Now, I suppose I'd better

get back upstairs to my room. We'll find a way to talk again tomorrow."

While she waited for Teresa, Jessie unpacked the saddle roll in which she'd brought her extra clothing from Santa Fe. She filled the china washbowl on her night table from the pitcher of water that stood beside it, and she took a quick sponge bath before putting on fresh clothing. She'd finished dressing and was standing beside the window, looking down through the fading daylight at the activity in the *placita*, when Teresa came in.

"I didn't intend to leave you alone for such a long time, Jessie," she apologized. "But Grandfather seemed lonely, and I thought I'd better stay with him for a while."

"I didn't mind at all," Jessie assured her. "I made good use of the time."

"Oh, we always have plenty of time here," Teresa said. "I think perhaps we have too much. But when I try to find something to do, Grandfather stops me and reminds me that well-born ladies have servants to do the work."

"He's very much of the old school, isn't he?"

"Completely, Jessie. But the entire Rio Arriba is a place where time has stood still. I'm not really sure that it'll ever change, either, as isolated as we are up here. But come on in my room while I change. We've still got a lot of talking to do, and dinner won't be served until eight o'clock."

Dinner had been a formal affair, served by white-jacketed youths from the *placita* under Bartolome's strict supervision. Don Esteban, Teresa, and Jessie had eaten by the light of a dozen candles burning in tall silver candelabras on a table that would have accommodated twenty people more. They had not gone to the table until the big grandfather clock in the hall had chimed eight, and it had just

101

struck eleven when Don Esteban rose and bowed to signify that the meal was over.

They were just turning away from the table and starting toward the door, when a scattered fusillade of shots sounded outside. One bullet ricocheted off the iron grillwork that covered the downstairs windows, and plowed a furrow across the polished surface of the dining table. The slug upset a wine glass and went on to shatter the decanter that stood beside it.

Jessie could hear the faint thudding of other shots striking the thick adobe walls of the hacienda. A crashing of glass sounded from the hall, and Teresa stifled a scream. Through the open door of the long dining room Jessie heard the screams of the women who were working in the kitchen.

"Cabalgadores de la noche!" Don Esteban exclaimed. He showed an agility that belied his years in striding from the table to the window and pulling aside the velvet drapes to peer into the darkness.

Teresa hurried to him, saying, *"Abuelito! Tenga cuidado!"*

Jessie turned and started toward the door. She called over her shoulder, "I'll go upstairs and get my rifle!"

Teresa had taken her grandfather's arm and was trying to pull him away from the window. When Jessie spoke, the old man said quickly, "There is no need to go upstairs. We have rifles ready in the hallway. Come!"

Ki was hurrying down the long hall toward the dining room as they went through the door. He carried his rifle, and when he saw the three he asked, "What's happening, Jessie?"

"Don Esteban says we're being attacked by night riders," she replied. "There are guns somewhere here in the hall. Do what you can, Ki, while we get them!"

After the first ragged volley, the shots from the attackers

had become spaced out but continued steadily. The sharp crack of rifles and the faint plop of shots hitting the hacienda's thick adobe walls were underlined by the muffled thudding of hoofbeats as the night riders circled the building.

Don Esteban had hurried along the hall to a door. He opened it and revealed a dozen modern Winchesters racked in a shallow, closetlike room.

"All of them are loaded and ready," the old man said. "And there is ammunition in plenty here on the shelves below them."

Ki had already disappeared into the dining room. Jessie heard his rifle bark, its nearby report easily distinguished from the muffled sounds of the firing from outside the house. Don Esteban pushed past Jessie, heading for the front door. He carried his rifle like one accustomed to using it, and Jessie realized that in spite of his age the old man could still hold his own in exchanging shots with the attackers.

Teresa was grabbing one of the weapons from the rack, and now she picked up another and passed it to Jessie.

"Come to the parlor with me," Teresa said. "We can take care of that side of the house while Grandfather and Ki defend the others."

Bartolome appeared at the rear end of the hall, running toward them. As he passed them on his way to the gun closet, he gasped, "I had to see that the women in the kitchen were safe, Senorita Teresa." He looked down the hall toward the entry way, where Don Esteban was thrusting his rifle through a porthole that he'd opened in the massive front door, and went on, "I will join Don Esteban and see to his safety, too."

Jessie followed Teresa into the parlor. The heavy velvet drapes at one of its high windows were billowing in the night wind that blew through a shattered pane, and Teresa ran to it at once. Jessie started toward a more distant window, and an instant before she reached it, its glass crashed and broke and a slug tore through the drapes.

Jessie dropped to the floor and crawled to the window, where she pushed the drapes aside with the muzzle of her rifle. She peered into the darkness, broken now by a few lights that were showing from the *placita*. Seeing the dim form of a rider and his horse, she snapped off a shot. The horse broke stride but did not fall, and before Jessie could aim again the rider was out of sight around the corner of the house.

Muzzle flashes began breaking the darkness from the *placita* now, brighter than the lights that trickled from the houses, their reports cracking through the night. Jessie's eyes adjusted to the blackness that shrouded the strip between the hacienda and its encircling wall, but she found no targets.

She was suddenly aware that the thrumming of hoofbeats was no longer loud and close, but had begun to fade into silence. There was no more shooting from the attackers, and the muzzle flashes from the *placita* had also stopped cutting the darkness.

In the settling silence, Teresa called, "We don't have to worry anymore, Jessie. The *cabalgadores* have gone."

Chapter 10

"Gone?" Jessie echoed. "But—they just started shooting ten or fifteen minutes ago!"

"That is their way," Don Esteban said from the doorway. He came into the parlor, followed by Ki. Both still carried their rifles. Don Esteban went on, "You must understand, Miss Starbuck, these are not serious raids."

"They were firing real bullets at us," Jessie reminded him. "And that's serious enough for me."

"Oh, we're used to night riders," Teresa put in. "We don't enjoy them, but neither are we afraid of them."

"They usually do very little harm," Don Esteban said. He turned to Bartolome. "What is the damage this time?"

"Two large windows in the dining room, *patrón*. And one in here, I see. They did not attack the *placita* this time," the steward replied.

"Then you will attend to the repairs as usual," Don Esteban said. "There are extra panes of glass in the storehouse, I suppose?"

"Of course, *patrón*. The broken panes will be replaced

tomorrow morning. I will also look at the walls then, and see if there are holes that must be plastered."

"Good." The old man nodded. "Now, before you go to the *placita* to inspect the damage there, you will please bring us a decanter of the oldest *relámpago de Taos*. A few swallows will go down well after our experience."

As Bartolome bowed himself out, Jessie picked up her interrupted conversation with the old man. "You don't seem to be upset about the attack, Don Esteban. Is that because you are raided often by these night riders?"

"As I told you, the night riders are not serious," he replied calmly. He sat down in one of the ornate high-backed armchairs and gestured for the others to be seated while he went on. "These sudden raids in the darkness are made only to do enough damage to keep us busy here at the hacienda while others of the outlaws steal our cattle or sheep. Tomorrow or the day after we will get word from the herders that a few animals have been stolen from the cattle range or the sheep pastures."

"And you don't take the rustling seriously?" Jessie asked.

"My dear Miss Starbuck, when I have ten thousand sheep and several thousand head of cattle, of what importance are ten or twenty animals?" Don Esteban shrugged. "It is a tribute we pay, like the taxes that go to the government of the territory."

"Well, that's one way to look at it, I suppose," Jessie answered with a frown. "But if this had happened on the Circle Star, I'd have a bunch of my men out right now trying to find the rustlers."

"You couldn't be expected to understand unless you'd been born in the Rio Arriba, as I was, Jessie," Teresa said. "But maybe Grandfather can explain to you about them."

"These rustlers, as you call them, are our own people," the old grandee told Jessie. "They are men who have been

106

forced to become fugitives because of your laws. Do we not owe them something, when we have so much and they have so little?"

Ki had listened in silence. Now he asked, "You're not going to chase them and try to punish them?"

"Of course not." Don Esteban shook his head. "If we did that, they might be driven to even worse acts."

"That's the doctrine of Buddha, which my mother's people follow!" Ki explained. "Do not seek revenge on your enemies; respect the right of all creatures to live."

Don Esteban looked at Ki as though seeing him for the first time. "Then, you are not Indian?" he asked.

Before Ki could answer, Teresa said quickly, "Ki's mother was Japanese. His father was an American."

"And if you've been thinking of him as a servant, he isn't that, either," Jessie added before Don Esteban could speak. "Ki is my trusted companion and friend, as he was my father's."

Don Esteban's eyes widened. He said soberly, "I have been guilty of a misconception! Forgive me for assuming too much, Miss Starbuck. I did not think to ask you of Ki's position." He turned back to Ki and said, "I will tell Bartolome to move you to the lower floor and to set a place for you at our table."

"It's not necessary to move me, Don Esteban," Ki replied. "I'm comfortable where I am. But I will join you at meals."

Bartolome came in balancing a silver tray that held several wine glasses and a crystal decanter with an almost colorless liquid. He set the tray on the table in the middle of the room and looked inquiringly at Don Esteban.

"That is all," the old man said. "Go now and see to the people at the *placita*. But I will have instructions to give you when you report back to me."

"Sí, patrón." Bartolome nodded and left.

Don Esteban rose stiffly and walked to the table. He moved carefully, as though his muscles and joints were protesting. In the slow manner of someone not accustomed to doing such things, he filled four glasses from the decanter and passed a glass to each of them.

Turning to Jessie, he explained, "This is a whiskey that we in the Rio Arriba call Taos lightning. It is made at a small ranch of mine near Taos, but it has been well aged, and I think you will find it welcome after the surprise and our exertions."

Raising his glass, he drained it with a single swallow. Jessie had no recourse but to follow her host's example. The liquor was smooth as she swallowed it, but after a few moments her throat began to burn. She exchanged glances with Ki, who was also keeping a straight face, though his eyes were watering.

When she was sure she could speak, Jessie said, "Your Taos lightning is excellent, Don Esteban, though I'll confess that I have no standard to judge it by. But if you'll excuse me now, I'm ready to go to bed. It's been a very busy day."

"Of course," he said. "And I can see that Teresa is tired, too. Rest well, both of you. Tomorrow, I will have a surprise for you."

Jessie swayed to keep her balance as the light covered carriage bounced over the narrow, rutted road. In any place except the Rio Arriba, she thought, the road would have been called a path or a trace. It was nothing more than a pair of shallow troughs cut in the hard red soil by wagon wheels, with a much deeper center rut beaten by horses' hooves.

Bartolome, holding the reins, sat beside Don Esteban in the front seat of the open carriage. Jessie, Ki, and Teresa were in the back. The trip was the surprise promised the previous evening by Don Esteban. At breakfast, he'd announced that the day would be devoted to a visit to Rioja.

"It is past time for Bartolome to order our supplies, and I must inform Gomez of the attack last night so that he can spread the word to the other ranchers," he'd explained. "But if you wish to rest, we can put off the trip."

"There's no need to change your plans," Jessie had told him. "I had all the rest I needed last night. And I'd enjoy seeing more of your beautiful country."

They'd set out after breakfast and for almost two hours had been jouncing over the rough road. It had not been a ride that encouraged conversation, though Teresa had occasionally called Jessie's attention to some special feature of the countryside: the rugged peaks of a distant mountain ridge thrusting above the horizon, their flanks bathed in the brilliant morning sunshine; a trail that led to one of the ranch's grazing grounds; a picturesque stand of pine trees standing alone on the side of a hill.

"There's Rioja ahead," Teresa said now, pointing to the dozen or so adobe buildings whose flat roofs rose above the crest of the slope they were climbing. "And just before we get to it, we'll leave our own land for the first time."

As they topped the upslope and started down into the little sheltered valley beyond the crest, Rioja came into full view. The small adobe houses, scattered higgledy-piggledy up the sides of the narrow valley, centered roughly around a larger building that Jessie readily identified as the store. Like the houses, it was built of adobe.

At one side of the store, in the building's shade, a half-dozen men stood laughing and talking. At the hitch rail in front of the store there were three horses and a pair of burros. To their side stood a high-wheeled *carreta,* as well as a handsome dappled gray hitched to a chaise that shone with a fresh coat of black enamel.

Indicating the chaise with a nod, Teresa asked her grandfather, "Do you want to drive on and come back later, *abuelito?*"

"Why should we?" he asked, his voice sharp. "We are certainly as welcome as the Hinojosas."

Turning to Jessie, Teresa explained. "The chaise belongs to Don Antonio Hinojosa. As I've told you, we are not the best of friends with his family."

"Whatever we think, they are at least civilized," Don Esteban said sternly. Turning to Bartolome, he went on, "We will stop as we had planned."

Bartolome reined in on the side of the hitch rail opposite the chaise and, after securing the reins, helped Don Esteban and the women to alight. The old grandee led the way to the store entrance. As they entered the store, the half-dozen men standing at its side turned to stare. After the bright sunshine, the interior of the store seemed dim, lighted as it was by only four narrow windows. For a moment, until her eyes adjusted, Jessie saw the occupants only as so many blurs.

Then her vision cleared and she had no trouble in identifying Don Antonio Hinojosa; though he was not as old as Don Esteban, his features had the same regal angularity. Beside him stood a younger man, and for a moment Jessie was sure that she'd again encountered Felipe Hinojosa. Then she noted subtle differences in the face of the man she was now seeing: more finely chiseled lips, a rounder jawline, a less sharply aquiline nose.

Neither of the old men extended his hand. The two stared soberly at one another, as though each was challenging the other to speak first. Hinojosa was the first to yield.

"Esteban." He nodded. "I trust you are in good health?"

"Very good indeed, Antonio," Don Esteban replied stiffly.

110

Yielding to convention, he went on, "I have the honor to present to you Miss Jessica Starbuck. She is visiting Teresa from Texas, where she has a large cattle ranch. The gentleman beside her is her assistant, Ki."

"*A sus órdenes, Señorita Starbuck, Señor Ki,*" Don Antonio said with a small half-bow. He indicated the young man beside him. "Allow me to present my son, Diego."

Diego Hinojosa shook Ki's hand, and they exchanged a few polite words, but when the young man turned to Jessie he did not settle for a bow as Don Antonio had. He stepped away from his father and extended his hand. And when Jessie grasped it, he bent over it and kissed her hand. Rising, he said, "I am most happy to meet you, señorita. You make the day brighter than it has been."

"Thank you," Jessie answered.

Diego turned to greet Teresa. "It has been a long time since we have seen each other, Teresa," he said. "Do you ever think of the days when we were children, you and Felipe and me, playing together so happily?"

"Now and then," she replied. "But we are not children anymore, and things have changed."

Ki said, "If you don't mind, Jessie, I'll go along with Bartolome while he's placing his order."

"Of course." She nodded, then turned back to Teresa and Diego, who had continued chatting about old times.

Don Esteban ignored the three younger people. He said to the elder Hinojosa, "Antonio, we must speak together for a moment." The two men took a step away, and Don Esteban continued, "I came to inform Morales that the night riders have returned, but since we have met—"

"They have attacked the Rancho Velarde?" Hinojosa broke in.

"Last night. The Rancho Almagre may be their next target."

"It could not have been a serious raid, or you would not be here," Hinojosa said, his brows knotting into a frown.

"It was not. A few shots at the hacienda, nothing more than a warning. They did not attack the *placita.*"

"I appreciate your consideration, Esteban," Don Antonio said, his voice now formal. "I will tell my *mayordomo* to post sentries for the next week or two."

Don Esteban nodded and turned back to the rest of the group. Jessie had joined Teresa and Diego in listening to the brief exchange between the two old men, and when it ended she realized with a start that Diego had not released her hand.

"Please, Don Diego," she said. "May I have my hand back? I would like to look around the store."

"Your hand is very strong—for a woman's," Diego told her, still holding it firmly.

Teresa broke in to say, "That's because Jessie is a strong woman. I'm sure you'd be surprised if you knew her full ability, Diego."

"Oh, Teresa!" Jessie protested. "Please!"

Teresa was not to be hushed. She went on, "Her ranch in Texas is only a bit smaller than those here in the Rio Arriba, and Jessie has run it by herself since her father's death."

"I am indeed impressed," Diego said. Turning back to Jessie, he said, "You are the first woman I have ever met who runs a ranch, Miss Starbuck. Perhaps you would like to visit our Rancho Almagre and give me your opinion of it."

"I'm here visiting Teresa to get a vacation from the Circle Star," Jessie said. "But thank you for the invitation."

"If you should change your mind . . ." Diego shrugged. With another small bow, he released Jessie's hand and turned

112

back to Teresa to say, "Perhaps you can persuade Miss Starbuck, Teresa. It's been a long time since you've visited Rancho Almagre."

"Yes. And I'm sure you know why," Teresa replied. "Grandfather and Don Antonio—"

Diego interrupted her. "Should make up their old quarrel and be friends again, as they were when we were children."

"They won't, as long as Felipe continues what Jessie—" She stopped quickly, but not soon enough to keep Don Antonio from hearing his other son's name.

"What is this regarding Felipe?" he asked Teresa.

"Nothing, Don Antonio," she replied.

"Nonsense!" he snorted. "Something he has done must have brought up his name."

Jessie sensed an argument brewing and tried to stop it, not realizing where her efforts might lead the conversation. She told Don Antonio, "Teresa was about to say that I met your other son while Ki and I were traveling from the sawmill to Rancho Velarde."

"You have met Felipe?" Diego asked. "He did not mention this to me."

"Nor to me," Don Antonio said.

Don Esteban's head had turned when he heard Felipe's name. He broke into the conversation to ask Jessie, "You said that when you met him you were on the way to the Rancho Velarde from the sawmill, did you not?"

"Yes. When Ki and I got on the wrong road, we met one of the men from the little settlement there, the place he called Big Piney. He guided us to the mill and set us on the right path."

"And along that path, did you not see a sign marking the boundary of the Rancho Velarde?" the old man went on.

"We saw—" Jessie stopped short as she realized what

her thoughtless remark had done. She tried to correct her error. "We met Don Antonio's son on the way to your ranch, Don Esteban."

"And the sign? Did you see it, also?" Don Esteban asked. When Jessie did not answer, he turned to Don Antonio. "Some of my men have reported seeing the remains of my boundary markers! Now I am sure it was Felipe who destroyed them. And I am equally sure that it was you who ordered him to do so!"

"Believe me, I have given Felipe no such instructions!" Don Antonio insisted. "If he had damaged your property—" He stopped and shook his head. "No," he went on. "Of course he has not. Felipe must only have removed some of the markers that were on land that rightfully belongs to me, not the Velardes!"

"Say instead, on land that you once sold to me and are now trying to steal from me!" Don Esteban snapped.

"Watch what you say, Esteban Velarde!" Don Antonio grated. "No man calls a Hinojosa a thief and lives to repeat it!"

Teresa stepped between the two old men. "Grandfather! This is no place to get into a dispute with Don Antonio! Please, let us go back home at once before things get worse!"

"Stand aside, Teresa!" Don Esteban said harshly. "This is a matter Don Antonio and I must settle between ourselves!"

"Settle it at another time and place, then!" she urged.

Diego stepped into the dispute. He took his father's arm and said, "Teresa is right, *mi padre*. We have finished our business here. Come, let's go home now. Perhaps you and Don Esteban will meet later at a more suitable place and discuss your differences."

"They are your differences too! Yours and Felipe's!" Don Antonio said.

"Then let us wait until Felipe is with us to discuss them, and perhaps he can tell us if there is even any reason for the matter of boundary signs to arise between us," Diego insisted. "For all we know, if Don Esteban's boundary markers have been disturbed, some of the rabble from the sawmill town may be to blame, not Felipe."

Don Antonio was silent for a moment; then he nodded. "You are right, Diego. We do need Felipe with us to discover the truth of the matter." He turned to Don Esteban. "After I have talked with both my sons, I will send you a message arranging a meeting. Does that satisfy you?"

Don Esteban had cooled off, too. He nodded. "I accept your offer. But let it be as soon as possible."

"I will not keep you waiting," Don Antonio promised. He nodded to Diego. "Come. We will return home now."

Diego started to say something, but when he saw the black scowl on his father's face, he bowed deeply to Jessie and Teresa and followed Don Antonio out of the store.

Don Esteban said to Jessie, "It is unfortunate that you have become involved in a dispute between our family and the Hinojosas, Miss Starbuck. If I had not insisted on coming in after seeing their carriage, it would not have happened."

"Disputes don't upset me, Don Esteban," Jessie replied. "As it is, I feel that I'm to blame. I brought up the subject of the boundary markers."

"No," the old man replied. "The marker you saw is just one of several that my *rancheros* have reported finding broken up. I have known this was happening for some time, but did not think that Felipe, the son of an *hidalgo*, would stoop so low."

"I'm sure there's more to the differences between you and the Hinojosas than just a few signs," Jessie said, trying to open the way to asking Don Esteban about the Big Piney settlement and the identity of the mysterious Creighton who was trying to buy out the settlers there. "If I'm not prying into matters that you'd prefer not to talk about, perhaps you'll tell me the whole story someday."

"Of course," he agreed readily. "I have nothing to hide from you or anyone else. I will tell you when we are back at the hacienda."

"Can we start soon, Grandfather?" Teresa asked. "All this arguing and angry talk has started my head aching."

"I have only a few more words to say to Morales, and must be sure that Bartolome has completed his affairs," Don Esteban said. "Why do you not go and sit in the carriage? The fresh air will probably make you feel better."

"I'll go with you," Jessie volunteered. "Ki will come out when Bartolome does." Taking Teresa's arm, she led her out of the store.

Chapter 11

When Jessie and Teresa got outside they stood for a moment in front of the store, blinking as the brilliant high-altitude sunlight struck their eyes. When they started for the carriage, Jessie noticed that the black chaise had left, as had the three men who'd been lounging outside the store, and the horses that had been at the hitch rail.

"I hope being out here in the fresh air will make you feel better, Teresa," Jessie said.

"It will," Teresa said. "And I don't really feel as badly as I made out to Grandfather. I just wanted to be sure that he wouldn't go on talking about our family *contienda*." She saw a look of puzzlement on Jessie's face and added, "A *contienda* is an argument that keeps dragging on. It's not quite as bad as a feud, but a little bit worse than just a fuss."

"I see," Jessie said.

They walked slowly toward the carriage, but before they were close enough to step up into its seat they heard hooves thunking on the hard soil behind the store and stopped to look around. A horse and rider dashed around the corner of the building, and as the rider reached them he reined in. Leaning forward in his saddle, he handed Teresa a slip of folded paper.

"For you alone, Señorita Velarde," he said, and before either Teresa or Jessie could speak, he dug his spurs into his horse's flanks and rode away at a gallop.

Their mouths still open in surprise, Jessie and Teresa stared at the rider as he galloped up the slope and disappeared beyond its crest.

Jessie was the first to recover. She asked, "What on earth are you up to now, Teresa?"

"Believe me, I'm not up to anything!" Teresa protested. "If I were, don't you think that's the first thing I would have told you yesterday?"

"Yes, I suppose so," Jessie agreed. "Well, let's get in the carriage, out of this blinding sun, and we can read your mysterious message together—unless you'd rather not share it with me."

"Even without knowing what it is, I'm sure I won't mind sharing it with you," Teresa told Jessie as they settled into the carriage seat. "But believe me, Jessie, I don't know what could be written on this any more than you—" She stopped abruptly as Don Esteban came out of the store. Ki and Bartolome were only a step behind him. Bartolome carried several parcels.

Teresa quickly tucked the partly unfolded paper into the neck of her dress and said, "I'm not sure about sharing this with Grandfather, Jessie. You and I will read it together just as soon as we get back to the hacienda and can be alone."

"Are you feeling better now, my dear?" Don Esteban asked Teresa as he hoisted himself stiffly into the front seat of the carriage. "If the motion of riding is going to bother you—"

"I'm much better, Grandfather," Teresa assured him. "It

118

was so close and stifling in the store that the bad air must have bothered me."

"Very good, then," the old man said. "We'll start back home." He turned and added, "And I haven't forgotten my promise to you, Miss Starbuck. I will explain why there is a bad feeling between the Velarde and the Hinojosa families as we ride."

Bartolome had been stowing his parcels in the small space behind the rear seat. He and Ki got in, and the carriage started up the gentle grade out of the shallow valley. After they'd ridden in silence for a half mile or so, Don Esteban turned in his seat and told Jessie, "Now I will answer what you have asked me. But I must warn you, it is not a happy story. Even Teresa has not heard all of it, though it concerns her very deeply."

"Why have you not told me the story before, Grandfather?" Teresa asked gently.

Don Esteban sighed. "I had hoped that our family's foolish errors and mistakes in judgment might not be exposed," he said. "Especially since the honor of more than just the Velardes is involved. But let me begin at the beginning."

"It goes back many years," the old *hidalgo* said. "To a time when I was but a young man, before I had inherited the Tierra Roja grant from my father, who had it from his father, and so on back through the years to the time when the king of Spain gave us the land."

"All went well with our family for a long time. The Tierra Roja, like most of the grants here in the Rio Arriba, was never a source of great riches, such as those on which gold or silver was mined, but in those days it was the only part of Spain's New World domain that produced fat beef cattle. The cattle brought in a steady stream of gold, and all the ranches in the Rio Arriba prospered.

"Then there was the trouble between Mexico and Spain.

119

I was little more than a baby then, too young to understand, but the Velarde men supported the king against the Indians who were trying to seize the Spanish lands here in America. As events turned out, we were on the losing side, but when the Indians took power they soon learned that there were too many of us who were of the pure Spanish strain for them to overlook.

For a moment Don Esteban was lost in remembering. "We suffered in many ways, though," he said finally. "Parts of our land grants were voided, we lost the best of our grazing range to the south of the Rio Arriba, and many more unpleasant things took place. But I will not spend time telling you of details. It is enough to say that when the Velarde family fell on bad times, we needed help."

"So you went to your neighbors?" Jessie asked when Don Esteban fell silent with a sigh. "And they were the Hinojosas?"

"Yes. But you must understand, Miss Starbuck, that even the dispute over who should rule the land had not destroyed our friendship with them. We had come to the Rio Arriba together, and fought side by side to tame the land—oh, it was a very rough land then, I have been told. I myself married a daughter of the Hinojosas." He looked at Teresa and said, "You did not know this, my child, for your grandmother died very young, and by the time you were born our good neighbors had come very close to becoming our enemies."

"You should have told me this before, Grandfather," Teresa said. "It would have made clear many things I've wondered about."

"It is not good to talk of some things, Teresa, even to one's children," Don Esteban said. "It was a natural thing that when we Velardes were forced to look for help—money, you understand—my father should turn to Don Eusebio

120

Hinojosa, the father of Antonio and brother of my wife. Of this, at the time, I knew nothing myself. My father held the belief that children of his house remained children as long as their father lived. He told us nothing of his business affairs. But I am getting away from my story.

"In the course of time and in the fullness of his years, my father died, and I became head of the house of Velarde. Only then did I learn of the old loan. As honor required, I went to Don Eusebio and told him I could not pay him, and he assured me that I need have no worry. 'It is a matter between *hidalgos*,' he said. 'I would not have my sister's husband embarrassed over a mere matter of money.' But he did not tell me that my father had guaranteed the loan with a mortgage deed to a large part of the Tierra Roja grant."

Again the old man stopped, and Jessie said, "You've never been able to pay off the loan, then?"

"Oh, the loan was paid," Don Esteban said quickly. He turned from Jessie to Teresa and went on, "Your father, Carlos, was a young and adventurous man at the time I speak of. He had gone to California when the great gold discoveries were made, and unlike so many adventurers he did find gold—much gold. He also found a wife from a good California family that had roots in Spain. That was your mother, Teresa. She was already carrying you in her womb when your father brought her home to the rancho."

"Then Carlos paid the money you owed the Hinojosas?" Jessie asked.

"To the penny, of course—with a chest full of gold," Don Esteban replied. "He did not know of the mortgage deed, nor did I. And Don Eusebio did not give him a receipt for the payment. I asked Carlos of this, and he said Don Eusebio had promised to observe the formalities in a few days. I took this to mean that he would call on us, and we would drink a glass of *relámpago de Taos* and then he would

121

hand us a receipt for the money Carlos had given him. It was the way things were done then between *hidalgos*, you understand."

"But something went wrong," Jessie said.

"More things than I wish to think of even now, Miss Starbuck. After Teresa was born, when her mother was able to go out again, she and Carlos went to attend a dance given by some friends in Taos. On their way home they were trapped by a *lleno furioso*, one of those great walls of water that rush down a dry arroyo without warning, from a storm in the mountains above. We found their poor, torn bodies far down the arroyo from the trail crossing many days later."

"But surely you went to Don Eusebio after you'd recovered from the shock of their deaths, and asked him about a receipt," Jessie said.

"We could not attend to business matters during the year of mourning," Don Esteban explained. "And in the fullness of his years, Don Eusebio died before the mourning period had passed. Then there was the year of mourning observed by the Hinojosa family. And after a decent time of waiting, when I went to ask Don Antonio about the receipt, he claimed that he knew nothing of the payment Carlos had made to his father."

"Have you talked to a lawyer about this, Don Esteban?" Jessie asked.

"We have a saying, Miss Starbuck. 'When a lawyer comes in your door, honesty goes out your window.' There are no lawyers in the Rio Arriba. I would have to go to Santa Fe to find one, and then the gossip would begin and our family would appear to be fools. No. It is better to settle disputes between our own kind with *pundonor*, our honor as *hidalgos*."

Jessie saw she'd be wasting words if she pointed out that the Velarde family's plight had been caused by the refusal

122

of the Hinojosas to observe the *hidalgo* code. Instead, she asked Don Esteban, "The Hinojosas didn't make any effort to interfere with affairs on the Tierra Roja grant until after you'd sold your forest land to the people at Big Piney, did they?"

"They did nothing when the Anglos came here, or when they built their sawmill. It was only when the man Creighton offered to buy their mill from the settlers at Big Piney that our trouble began," he replied.

"And Creighton came to you first?" she went on.

Don Esteban nodded. "Yes. After the settlers did not sell the mill and the forest land to him, he proposed that I drive them off. He offered me a great deal of money if I would do this. But the loggers have always paid me promptly; I could not dishonor the Velarde name by doing what he suggested."

"Then Creighton went to Don Antonio?"

"Somehow, he found out about the old debt which Don Antonio claims was never paid. That is when the present trouble began."

While Don Esteban had been telling his long story and answering Jessie's questions, the carriage had been making steady progress over the rutted road. The imposing bulk of the hacienda was visible now, and the old man fell silent. The others had little to say. Jessie had run out of questions, and Ki sat quietly reflecting on the vexing situation. Teresa was lost in silent thought, absorbing her newly learned family history.

Bartolome reined in at the door of the big house and hurried to assist the old man to alight. He asked, "You will want luncheon at the usual time, *patrón?*"

"Of course." Don Esteban was handing Teresa and Jessie out of the carriage. "Unless Miss Starbuck and Teresa would like to rest an extra hour."

"Don't worry about us, *abuelito,*" Teresa said. "We'll have a half hour to wash off the dust and stretch. Come on, Jessie. We'll go on upstairs and get ready."

As soon as she'd closed the door of her bedroom, Teresa was groping in her bodice for the slip of paper handed her by the rider in Rioja.

"This has been burning a hole in my skin," she told Jessie. "Even when I was listening to Grandfather's story about our family problems, I couldn't forget it."

"You hadn't heard what he told us?" Jessie asked.

Teresa shook her head. "I knew my father and mother had been killed by the *lleno* when I was just a baby," she said. "But I was never told about the gold he brought back from California, or the money Grandfather borrowed from the Hinojosas. It makes a lot of things clear that I'd wondered about, though." She was unfolding the creased slip of paper as she spoke. "No more questions now, Jessie. Not until we read this."

As Teresa smoothed out the paper, Jessie moved around to look over her shoulder. The half sheet was filled with closely written script, in Spanish. Teresa began reading, translating as she read.

"'My dear Teresa. I call on our old friendship to ask of you a great favor. At my first sight of your beautiful friend, I lost my heart to her. I must see her again and talk with her and tell her of my feelings. I cannot visit at your hacienda for reasons we both know too well. But you will remember the cave with the spring where we played as children. On the day after tomorrow, I beg you to bring Miss Starbuck there, so that we can become better acquainted. I will wait from noon onward, with trembling anticipation. Do not fail me in this, Teresa. Your friend from the days of childhood. Diego.'"

"Oh, my!" Jessie exclaimed. "What a romantic effusion! Trembling anticipation, indeed!"

"But he's serious, Jessie!" Teresa said. "I know Diego. Until I went east to school, we remained good friends in spite of the troubles between our families."

"You can't be suggesting that I meet him!"

"I don't want to suggest anything. You've got to be the one who decides," Teresa replied.

After a moment's thought, Jessie said, "I think I've grown past the stage of going to a cave, of all places, to meet a young man I've seen one time, and then only for a few minutes."

"You mean that Diego didn't 'strike any sparks,' as you used to say at Miss Booth's."

"I was quite a bit younger then. Perhaps I've lost some of my romantic dreams, Teresa. Haven't you?"

Jessie regretted her last two words the moment she'd said them, remembering Teresa's sad experience with the man to whom she'd been engaged. But she was surprised at her friend's reply.

"I did for a while, after Roger died. All I could think of was that I wanted to die too, so that I could be with him again. But after a while I realized that being united in heaven, as the church had taught me we would be, did not mean that we would be united as man and woman in the full way we had been before. And I know now that once a woman has learned the joy of being in bed with a man, she never loses her desire to let herself go in a man's arms. At least, I haven't. Have you?"

Jessie did not reply for a moment. Teresa's frank confession had reminded her of the wise old housekeeper, a former geisha who had assisted Alex with her upbringing. Among the things the old woman had said was, "When a man invites you to share his bed, you may be led by false modesty to refuse him. But you must always remember that your days of youthful joy are numbered, just as are the hairs on your head." Strangely, what Teresa had just told her seemed almost an exact echo of her teacher's words.

"You've grown very wise since I saw you last, Teresa," she said at last. "You're not at all the wide-eyed little girl at Miss Booth's who was so shocked at what I'd already learned about men and sex."

"I'm glad I'm not that girl any longer," Teresa replied. "But you haven't answered my question."

"No, I haven't lost my desire," Jessie assured her. "But your young friend Diego—"

"He was attracted to you very strongly," Teresa broke in, "or he wouldn't have left this note."

"Perhaps it's just a woman Diego's looking for. Not necessarily me, just any woman."

"Oh, Jessie!" Teresa smiled. "Do you think that because we live here in the Rio Arriba, where there are no towns, young men and women live purified lives?"

"I hadn't really thought about it," Jessie replied.

"Things on the Rancho Almagre are very much like they are here at our ranch. Every year we get four or five babies from the *placita,* and sometimes the mother isn't even sure who her child's father is."

"I suppose we'd have the same thing on the Circle Star if there were any women except me on the ranch. But I've learned to restrict my little flings to the times when I'm away from home."

"Which is exactly what you are now," Teresa reminded her.

"You think I should take Diego's invitation, then?"

"I'm not going to answer that, Jessie. It's not my choice to make. If it was, I think I'd meet him, though."

"And how would you explain to your grandfather?"

126

"I wouldn't, of course. But Grandfather doesn't know everything that I do here at the ranch, even if he thinks he does."

"You've become a scheming woman, then?"

"Of course not. At least, I don't think of myself as being one. But we go to Santa Fe and to Taos now and then. If I meet a man who attracts me and I want to meet him privately, I've found ways to arrange it."

"There's one thing that does bother me," Jessie said, frowning. "If I should meet Diego, and Don Esteban or Don Antonio found out about it, wouldn't it make the situation worse between your families?"

Teresa shook her head. "Nothing could make things worse between the Velardes and the Hinojosas, Jessie. If that's the only thing holding you back, don't worry about it for a minute."

Jessie was silent longer than she'd been at any time during their talk. At last she said, "All right, Teresa. I'll admit the idea didn't appeal to me at first, but I'll meet young Diego. I don't say I'll want to go any further than talking to him, but go ahead and arrange things."

Chapter 12

"I hope you don't have anything planned for Jessie and me to do tomorrow, Grandfather," Teresa told Don Esteban at dinner the evening after Jessie had given her consent to meet Diego.

"You have made plans of your own?" Don Esteban asked.

"Yes. I thought she'd like to see something of the country to the east. The wooded country and the mountains are so different from the part we saw yesterday, when we went to Rioja."

"As you please, of course," the old *hidalgo* replied. "I suppose you've already made arrangements with Bartolome for your luncheon and horses?"

"I've arranged everything I can think of," Teresa assured him. "And if you would like to come with us—"

"No, indeed," Don Esteban answered. "You know the country almost as well as I do, and I'm sure you two still have a great deal to talk about that would be of small interest to an old man like me. Besides, a day on horseback no longer appeals to me."

"We won't leave until midmorning, and we'll be back in plenty of time for dinner," Teresa said quickly.

"Enjoy your outing, then," Don Esteban said. "The Rio Arriba hills are very beautiful at this time of the year."

"After you told Don Esteban we'd be riding tomorrow, I had an idea," Jessie told Teresa as they started up the stairs to her rooms after dinner.

"Does that mean you've changed your mind about Diego?"

"No. But there are some things about Big Piney that I'm still interested in finding out. Suppose we ask Ki to go with us, and you two can ride down there while I'm—well, talking with Diego."

"You don't mind Ki knowing you're going to meet Diego?"

"Of course not," Jessie replied. "There aren't any secrets between me and Ki. We don't tell one another everything we do, of course, but as I've explained before, Ki is my friend and helper, not my lover."

"Why are you so interested in Big Piney, Jessie? It's just a dozen or so houses and a sawmill."

Jessie didn't want to try to explain to Teresa about the international cartel and the unceasing struggle between her and its sinister forces. Instead she said, "You know my father left me a number of businesses to look after, Teresa. Lumbering is one of them. I have one large lumber mill on the Pacific coast and another in the northern part of Idaho, near the Canadian border. I thought perhaps—"

Teresa broke in excitedly, "You're thinking about buying the sawmill at Big Piney, aren't you? Oh, Jessie, it would be wonderful if you did! Then you'd come here more often, and we wouldn't have to keep in touch just by letters!"

"Now, don't jump to conclusions," Jessie cautioned. "You know someone else is trying to buy the mill."

"Of course I do! That man you were asking Grandfather about, the one who tried to buy the Big Piney land from him. Creighton was his name."

"Yes. And I'd like to know a lot more about him, Teresa. That's why I thought you and Ki might be able to help me by going over there. The people at Big Piney have met Ki, but I'm sure they've known you a lot longer. I'd like Ki to go, too, because he knows the kind of questions to ask."

"I think it's a wonderful idea, Jessie! Riding with Ki to Big Piney will give me something to do while you're with Diego. And ask Ki to go, by all means!"

Though Jessie and Ki had traveled over part of the western section of the Tierra Roja grant on their way to the ranch, they had not been as far north as the faint trail Teresa led them to. In contrast to the gentle, grass-covered hills and hollows of the eastern section, the western area was broken land, the beginning of the high, forested mountains they could see to the north as they rode through the warm air of late morning.

In some parts of the rough up-and-down terrain the trail was dim, almost obliterated, but Teresa did not hesitate. The sun had just slid past its zenith when she reined in and told Jessie, "You can find your way easily from here. About a half mile ahead there is a steep cliff. Ride north along its base and you will see the mouth of the cave. If Diego isn't there yet, he'll surely be along soon."

"Shall I wait at the cave for you and Ki?" Jessie asked.

"That would be best." Teresa turned to Ki. "An hour before sundown, do you think? Then we can be back at the hacienda well before dark."

"I'm sure we'll be through at Big Piney in time to get back by then," Ki agreed. "As I remember, the mill's not more than another hour's ride from here."

They parted then. Jessie rode along the base of the cliff, wondering from time to time why she was going to a place she'd never seen before to keep a rendezvous with a man she'd barely met. Curiosity, as well as the occasional stirrings of desire she felt after her long period of isolation on the Circle Star, kept her moving ahead.

She saw the mouth of the cave several minutes before she reached it, a narrow black triangle in the face of the towering stone wall. There was no horse tethered outside, and she wondered if she might not be riding on a fool's errand, until she saw Diego step from the black opening and gaze down the trail. He saw her at the same time and waved. Jessie reached the mouth of the cave, and he hurried to hold her stirrup while she dismounted.

"I was afraid you'd changed your mind," Diego said, looking into her eyes as they stood side by side. "But I would have waited until dark before giving up this chance to be with you."

"Your note was such a surprise that I thought you and Teresa might be playing a joke on me," Jessie said with a smile.

"Oh, no!" he said quickly, taking her hand. "From the first minute I saw you, I knew that I had to find a way to be with you, far from anyone else."

As she studied Diego's face, Jessie changed the first hasty impression she'd gotten of him in their brief meeting at the store. He was not as young as she'd taken him to be; she judged now that he was only a few years younger than she was. His head was bare, his straight jet-black hair glistening in the sun's bright rays. Though his tall frame made him look slightly built, his shoulders were broad and his torso sturdy. The smile that had formed when he saw Jessie softened his angular face, parting his full lips to give her a glimpse of even white teeth.

Taking the reins from her hand, Diego went on, "I'll lead your horse inside and tether it with mine. There's not much chance anyone will be passing, but it would be foolish to draw attention by leaving it out here."

Inside, the cave widened into a deep cavern, its top lost in darkness. A layer of fine sand covered the floor. Just inside the entry, the light trickling in through the mouth created an area of brightness that faded a few yards back into a soft, dusky twilight and, deeper in the cave, into inky blackness. Diego led Jessie's horse a short distance into the cavern to where his own mount stood, and there he dropped the reins and put a large stone on them.

"Come now," he said, taking her hand. "We have little enough time; let's make the most of it."

"What first gave you the idea that I might spend time with you?" Jessie asked, as Diego led her to the opposite side of the cave, stopping where a large, thick Navajo blanket had been spread on the sandy floor beside a pair of saddlebags. "We said only a few words to each other there at the store."

"I didn't know that you would," he replied. "I only hoped. But—" He shrugged, then picked up the saddlebags and took out a bottle. "I looked into your eyes and saw that you are a woman who does not know fear, a strong woman who relishes adventure." He pulled the cork from the bottle and handed it to Jessie. "Have you tasted our Taos lightning?"

"Once. Don Esteban served some after the night rider attack the other night." Jessie tipped the bottle and sipped. As she handed the liquor back to Diego, she went on, "I suppose I'm also a curious woman, or I wouldn't be here."

Diego took a swallow from the bottle and set it aside. "We don't need this, do we, Jessie?"

When she shook her head, he cradled her chin in his hand and bent to kiss her. It was the first kiss of passion

Jessie had experienced in several months, and she responded to the questing tongue tip that Diego slipped between their clinging lips with a thrust of her own tongue.

Without breaking their kiss, they sank down on the blanket. Diego let his hand slip from Jessie's chin to stroke the soft, sensitive skin of her throat, then followed the stroking of his fingers with his warm, moist lips while his hand moved down to cup her breast.

For a moment he was content to caress the tender globe through the thin fabric of her blouse, but soon she felt him fumbling at the buttons. As though moving of its own accord, Jessie's hand had been brushing over Diego's chest, but she stopped to push his clumsy fingers aside and quickly unbutton the blouse. He pulled the opened placket apart, and his fingers sought the sensitive buds of her bared breasts.

Jessie arched her back as Diego began stroking the firm rosettes with his fingertips. Her hand resumed its stroking of his chest, moving slowly downward. Just as Diego broke their kiss, bending to caress the tips of her breasts with his warm lips, Jessie slid her hand between their close-pressed bodies, gently brushing the evidence of his desire with her cupped hand.

Diego interrupted his caresses to raise his head and whisper, "We have too many barriers between us. It's time to get rid of them, don't you agree?"

"Yes," Jessie replied in the same low tone. "And quickly."

They broke their embrace, and while Jessie shrugged off her blouse and slid her skirt down over her hips and thighs, Diego quickly shed his clothes as well. Jessie had worn no pantalettes to the rendezvous, and once free of the skirt, she levered out of her boots. She looked up to see Diego push his trousers down, and she gasped when she saw his swollen manhood free.

"I'm ready for you, Diego," she said softly.

Diego stood above her for a moment, gazing in admiration at Jessie's body. Her soft white skin glowed in the half-light that trickled into the cavern, and the pink tips of her full breasts were still pebbled from his tongue's caresses. The narrow vee of feathery hair above Jessie's rounded thighs was the hue of dark golden honey.

"You are very beautiful, my Jessie," he said, dropping to his knees beside her. "Even more beautiful than I dreamed."

Jessie smiled and raised her arms to pull him down to her. Diego yielded eagerly, and as their lips met she opened herself to him and guided him into the part of her that waited, moist and quivering, for his entry.

She gasped as Diego plunged into her, and exhaled a satisfied sigh as she felt his first deep penetration fill her. For a few moments they lay motionless, content just to be joined with the firm fleshly bond. Diego began stroking before their first sensations ebbed, long, measured, rhythmic thrusts that Jessie matched with gentle undulations of her hips.

After her long abstinence, Jessie did not hold back. She let herself rise quickly to a climax, confident by now that her lover was experienced enough to understand her need.

When he felt her begin to tremble, Diego brought his lips to her ear and whispered, *"Sí, querida, sí."*

Jessie let herself be carried up as Diego continued his rhythmic stroking. She cried out and clasped him tighter, his bare flesh smooth against hers, her body tossing and her hips rising and falling in ever-quicker spasms as she rode her crest.

Her cries of pleasure broke the stillness as her head tossed from side to side and her back arched convulsively, but Diego continued his long, forceful strokes. When Jessie's shudders ebbed, then ended, and she lay quiet, he slowed his stroking to the deliberate tempo with which he'd begun,

134

but he did not stop completely. Jessie lay quietly, waiting, her eyes closed, knowing that in a few moments Diego's unflagging thrusts would rouse her again.

Jessie was not disappointed in her lover, nor in her own capacity to respond. Diego's warm lips sought hers again, and once more their tongues entwined. His steady stroking began bringing Jessie to arousal, and Diego understood the meaning of her renewed response.

"Wait for me this time, *querida*," he whispered. "Let us share our pleasure now."

Jessie did not reply, but pulled him to her more tightly, and as her fervor grew she began rotating her hips each time she brought them up to meet him. She felt Diego's body begin growing taut, and now Jessie took the initiative. Clasping her hands around Diego's hips, Jessie started pulling them to hers each time he drove in.

Her gesture seemed to stimulate him, for he started thrusting with trip-hammer speed, quick lusty strokes that soon brought Jessie to the trembling brink of another climax. She held back in spite of her urgent shudders, until Diego's lunges grew ragged and erratic and his muscles tautened.

Jessie waited until she sensed that he could no longer hold back, and as Diego thrust with a final frenzied lunge, she let go her control. Their cries mingled in the quiet air of the cave and echoed from its walls as the crescendo that was shaking their bodies reached its peak. Then the cries faded and their tremors ebbed and stopped, and they lay entwined in silent fulfillment.

"You're a wonderful lover, Diego," Jessie whispered.

"It is your beauty and passion that inspire me," he replied, his voice soft. "Rest quietly now until our strength returns. We will find even greater satisfaction when we resume our caresses."

• • •

Even before Ki and Teresa were within sight of Big Piney, the shrill, rasping shriek of the sawmill reached their ears. They'd talked very little during the ride. Now and then Teresa pointed out a deer trail, or a view of distant mountains visible only for a few moments as the travelers topped a rise or entered a clearing. Occasionally they passed a spot that caused her to recall a childhood memory. They'd been riding on a downslope for a half hour or more, the incline that led to the river valley, and the trail was no longer straight, but wound between the boles of the towering trees.

"We're almost there, I think," Teresa said as the high-pitched shriek of the saw biting into a log reached their ears again. "It's been quite a while since I rode over here last, and either I don't remember landmarks or the trail's been changed."

"If we can hear the sawmill, we've got to be pretty close," Ki pointed out. "And I can see the sun reflected off water between those trees over there on the left."

They saw the settlement within a few moments, its cabins scattered beyond the belt of stumps. Ki rode directly to the sawmill and, as he'd hoped, found both Mike Burns and Tim Boyd inside. A log was just beginning its passage to the saw run, and Boyd signaled to Burns to throw the lever that diverted the current from the millrace. The log stopped before the huge steel saw bit into it, and the lumbermen walked over to greet Ki and Teresa.

Ki introduced them to Teresa, but the moment he mentioned her last name their faces froze into hard-set lines. Turning to Ki, Boyd said coldly, "I guess Miss Starbuck changed her mind about helping us, figured she wouldn't want to go against her old friends, them Velardes."

"You misjudge Jessie," Teresa broke in. "And you mis-judge my grandfather, too. He did not expect Don Antonio Hinojosa to behave as he is doing. Grandfather would never

136

stoop to any kind of underhanded action! He is—"

Boyd interrupted her. "Well, now, I can't blame you for sticking up for your grandpa, Miss Velarde. I'd do the same thing for my blood kin. But facts is facts, and the fact is he got us in a mess."

"Boyd's right," Mike Burns broke in. "It's easy for your grandpapa to blame somebody else, Miss Velarde. But I figger you rich folks is all in cahoots. You just work together, trying to squeeze out people like us."

"Please listen to us for a minute," Ki said. "Don Esteban told us the complete story. He says his son Carlos paid off that mortgage the Hinojosas had on this land. Don Antonio promised Carlos a receipt but didn't deliver it. Carlos is dead now, and as long as Don Antonio sticks to his story, there's not anything Don Esteban can do about it."

"What about the Johnny-come-lately that started all this ruckus, this Creighton?" Boyd demanded. "Seems like us folks is sorta caught in the middle."

"Miss Starbuck's wondering about him, too," Ki replied. "That's one reason Teresa and I came to Big Piney today, to find out if he's been around since we stopped here."

"None of us folks has seen hide nor hair of him," Burns said. "We been sorta wondering too."

"I guess it's a good thing you and Miss Velarde come here today, Ki," Boyd said. "Because after you and Miss Jessie left, we got our heads together and decided it was time to put up or shut up. We wrote a letter to Don Antonio Hinojosa and told him we wasn't going to sell out, and we wasn't going to let him or that Creighton run us off, either."

"Have you gotten a reply from him?" Ki asked.

Boyd shook his head. "Not yet. But we didn't send him the letter till the day after you and Jessie passed through."

"How did you send the letter to Don Antonio?" Teresa asked.

"Eddie—that's Joe and Betty Densmore's boy—he took it to the Hinojosa place," Boyd answered. "But when he tried to hand it to the old man, the flunky wouldn't let him inside, said he'd see the old man got the letter."

"I'm sure the servant at the Hinojosa ranch must have told Eddie the truth," Teresa said. "But he wouldn't have had time yet to reply. You must understand, Mr. Boyd, here in the Rio Arriba we do not move quickly on matters of business. Wait until you get a reply to your letter; then you can decide what you should do next."

Without warning, a rifle cracked somewhere upslope among the pine trees, and the slug raised a puff of dirt from the soil near Ki's feet. All of them turned to look for the source of the shot. They saw the shadowy figures of a half-dozen men dodging from tree to tree, approaching the settlement. One of them stopped and raised a rifle.

Ki grabbed Teresa and swung her around to the nearest of the high tree stumps as the rifleman fired. Boyd and Burns were running for the cover of the nearest stumps, too, and the doors of houses in the settlement were popping open, the women peering out to find out what the shooting was about.

Tim Boyd was crouching behind a stump only a few feet from the one where Ki and Teresa had taken cover. His voice grim, he said, "It looks like Don Antonio Hinojosa got our letter, Miss Velarde. And them rifle slugs is his answer!"

Chapter 13

Shots were now cracking regularly from the forested slope. The handful of Big Piney men who'd been working logs in the millpond or stacking the sawn boards were running from the mill, dodging from one stump to the next as they headed for their cabins to get weapons.

"What're we going to do, Ki?" Teresa asked.

"Don't worry," Ki assured her. "We're in better shape than those men on the slope are."

"I don't see how you can say that! You don't have a gun, and I don't either. Even if I had one, I'm not a very good shot."

"All the Big Piney men have rifles," he replied. "They'll be shooting back as soon as they get them." Turning, he called to Boyd, "How many men do you have?"

"Five, not counting me and Mike. Most of the boys is scattered out in the woods today, cutting trees."

"They can't get here in time to help, then," Ki said.

"Not likely. But now that them fellows that's gone after their rifles can cover us, me and Mike will go get ours.

Then we'll give these bastards what for!"

As Burns and Boyd ran toward the cabins, the attackers suddenly slackened their firing. Peering around the stump that shielded him and Teresa, Ki saw why the rifle shots had tapered off. The raiders were advancing.

Watching the roughly dressed men of the attacking force, Ki gave them credit for using good tactics. They'd formed a skirmish line in a shallow arc and were dodging from tree to tree, exposing themselves as little as possible in their advance down the slope. Ki took this as an indication that, whoever they were, the group assaulting the settlement had faced hostile fire before. He watched the men as they moved from one tree trunk to the next, marking their positions in his memory.

"Get ready to run to that cabin," he told Teresa, pointing to the little log house that stood nearest them. "After you're inside, I'll help Boyd and his men run the raiders off."

"What can you do without a rifle?" she asked.

"Guns aren't everything," Ki assured her.

Ki looked back at the settlement. He could see the muzzles of rifles sticking out from the corners of several cabins now, as the men who'd been caught in the mill by the surprise attack took up positions behind the thick log walls of their homes. Ki waited until they started firing and the attackers scrambled to take cover.

"We'll make a run for it now," he told Teresa. "It's as good a time as any. Come on!"

Grabbing Teresa's hand, half-pulling her behind him, Ki darted toward the cabin he'd picked out. They reached it before the raiders had had a chance to send a single shot after them. The cabin door was ajar, a woman peering out the crack. She saw Ki and Teresa and opened the door wider. Ki pushed Teresa toward the cabin.

"Go on in," he told her. "You'll be all right inside."

Before she could answer him, Ki started back up the slope. Calling on his warrior skills, he dropped to all fours and scampered in a zigzag line up the gentle slope. His years of disciplined training enabled him to move swiftly in spite of his awkward posture. He set his course in a wide arc roughly parallel to the curved line the attackers had now established, but fifty yards behind the raiding party. As he ran, Ki selected the tree he would use for cover. He reached it and pressed himself against the rough bark long enough to take several *shuriken* from a pocket of his leather vest.

A single quick glance pinpointed Ki's objective, and he wasted no time in getting to it. The man he'd decided on was just beyond accurate throwing range, and Ki began a second, more subtle approach. He flattened himself on the ground, his black vest and dark trousers making him almost indistinguishable from the heavy patches of shadow cast by the trees as the sun's rays filtered through the pine branches.

Wriggling forward, his eyes flicking from the terrain he was crossing to his target, Ki closed the gap between him and the raider. He stopped at a spot behind the man, close enough now to reach him with an accurate throw, and rose to his knees to launch a *shuriken* with a quick flick of the wrist.

As the star-shaped blade whirled silently to its target, Ki flattened himself on the ground again. The *shuriken* bit into the neck of the raider behind the tree, and the man cried out in pain as its razor edges sliced into the long muscle at the base of his neck and pierced the artery below it.

Letting his rifle fall to the ground, the attacker raised his hands to grasp the *shuriken*. He yelled again as the keen edges of the star points cut into his palms and fingers, but the cry ended in a choking gasp as the spurting blood drained from the artery and he collapsed in a silent heap.

Ki had been so certain of his target that he did not wait

to watch the effect of his blade. He glanced ahead, saw that the two men closest to him were concentrating their attention on the cabins, and decided that it was safe for him to run again to get the raider nearest him within range. He was behind all the raiders now, and their attention was still focused on the cabins. The distance he had to cover was small, and Ki decided to risk safety for speed. Levering to his feet, he ran quickly ahead until he was again within throwing range of a raider.

As he ran, Ki caught a fleeting glimpse of the way the fight was going. Battle-wise war veterans to a man, the defenders of Big Piney were holding their attackers to a stalemate. They did not make targets of themselves, but sheltered behind their cabins and popped out to shoot with rifles aimed and ready. If a shot did not hit its target, the slug tearing into the tree kept the attacker behind it from aiming carefully.

Dropping to the ground when he reached the spot he'd chosen, Ki launched his second *shuriken*. It was as effective as the first, though he'd picked a more exacting target. He had to spin the blade in low, almost from ground level, at an angle that brought it sailing upward between the rifleman's shoulder and his hatbrim.

One point of the whirling star dug into the vulnerable triangle between cheekbone and skull and sliced into the raider's brain. His body jerked into a backward bow, and his rifle fell from his nerveless hands as he collapsed. The man was dead before he hit the ground.

As the raider toppled, a cry sounded far upslope. Ki had paid little attention to that area; his targets had all been between him and the cabins. Rising to his knees, Ki looked up the slope. Two raiders sat their horses among the trees, but he could not see them clearly because of the big pine boles.

142

"Get the hell outa here, you fools!" one of the horsemen shouted. "Them damn squatters have already got you beat!"

In the area between Ki and the lake, a half-dozen men came from behind the concealing trees and began running upslope. To see them better, Ki stood up, confident that the fleeing raiders would pay no attention to him. He started dodging between the big pines on a course that paralleled theirs, trying to reach a spot where he could get a clear look at the horsemen.

They'd begun to turn their horses when he reached a gap in the forest, but in the fleeting glimpse he got before they were again hidden from view, Ki recognized one of them: Felipe Hinojosa. The second man, thickset and red faced, was a stranger.

From the cabins, Ki heard Tim Boyd shout, "Hold your places, boys! Don't try to chase 'em! They'll have horses waiting for 'em; you'll just be wasting your time!"

Ki had already made that decision. He started back to the settlement, pausing to retrieve his *shuriken* as he passed the bodies of the two raiders he'd brought down. The people in Big Piney were gathered into a group at the edge of the cabins when he got there. Teresa burst from the little knot of men and women and ran to greet him.

"I didn't believe you when you said you'd run them off, Ki," she told him. "How did you—"

"Later, Teresa," he said quickly, and started working his way through the group to where Boyd and Burns were standing.

"I don't know what it was you done upslope there, but it sure worked," Burns said. "I wish you'd tell me—"

"Another time, Mike," Ki broke in. "I've got a question for you. Is Creighton a big man, red faced, running to fat?"

"That's him," Burns said.

"You mean you seen him?" Boyd asked.

143

"Not only him, but Felipe Hinojosa," Ki replied. "They stayed clear of the fighting, but Creighton was giving orders to the men who were down here doing the shooting."

"Well, that don't surprise me none," Boyd said. "Now I guess we better—"

"Wait," Ki interrupted, glancing at the declining sun. "Just stay here and wait. It's too late in the day for you to do anything now, and I need to tell Jessie what I've found out."

Boyd hesitated for a moment, then nodded. "You and Miss Starbuck's been on our side from the day we seen you, Ki. I reckon we'd be better off doing what you say."

"We'll be back tomorrow—at least one of us will," Ki told him. He turned to Teresa. "Let's go meet Jessie. We've got a lot of things to talk about, the three of us."

"Our afternoon has been my life's most beautiful experience, *querida,*" Diego whispered in Jessie's ear. "If I had not spent these hours with you, I would not have believed that there was a woman like you in the world."

They were lying on the blanket side by side, Jessie's head on Diego's shoulder, his arms enfolding her, his hands cradling her breasts. Both of them were drained by the hours they'd spent in almost uninterrupted fervent embraces. There had been times in the past when Jessie had used the lessons she'd been taught by her geisha instructress, but never could she remember having shared them with a more ardent partner.

Jessie stirred and Diego reluctantly released her. She sat up and looked out the mouth of the cave. From the angle of the shadows cast by the few low-growing shrubs on the ground outside, she saw that the afternoon was far advanced.

"I'll have to get ready to leave," she told Diego. "Ki and Teresa have surely started back by now."

144

"I don't want our day to end," he said, a plea in his voice. "I want time to stand still for us!"

"I've enjoyed our time together too, Diego," she said. "But it's getting late. Ki and Teresa will be getting here soon, and we must get back to the Rancho Velarde before dark."

"Tomorrow, then?" he asked.

Jessie shook her head. "I can't promise. If Don Esteban has planned something for us to do, I wouldn't be able to beg off."

"Then the next day?"

"We'll see. I'm sure Teresa can get a message to you if I find I'll be free."

"Don't bother sending a message," he told her. "I'll come here about the time I did today and wait for you."

"And if I can't meet you?"

"Then I'll wait the next day, and the next, until you do come back."

Jessie kneeled beside Diego and planted a light kiss on his cheek, then stood up. She said, "It's very romantic for you to say things like that, my dear, but be more practical. Don't come and wait for me until I've sent word I'll be here."

Jessie picked up her skirt and blouse and dressed quickly, then slid her feet into her boots. Diego began dressing more slowly, his reluctance showing in every move.

Jessie watched him for a moment, then started toward the opposite side of the cave where the horses were tethered. The westward-moving sun had changed the angle of the light entering the cave. The wall where the horses stood had been in deep shadow earlier, but its full length was now almost completely visible. Only the last few yards, where the two sides of the cave converged into a sharp vee, was still shadowed. At the very edge of the area where light and

145

shadow merged, Jessie saw a bulky object she hadn't noticed before.

"What is this, Diego?" she asked, starting to walk toward her discovery.

Diego looked, stopped dressing, and started toward her. "I don't know," he said. "There's never been anything in this cave before, but I haven't been here for several months."

As they walked together toward the strange object, its outlines grew clearer. They saw that it was a small chest, bound with iron straps and secured with a massive padlock. They stopped in front of it, and Diego shook his head.

"I haven't any idea what that's doing here," he said. "I certainly didn't bring it here."

"And it can't have been brought in lately," Jessie told him, indicating the sandy floor of the cave, which bore no fresh footprints except their own.

"That's right," Diego agreed. "Footprints last a long time in this cave."

He stepped up to the chest and tugged at the padlock, then tried to pull the chest away from the wall. It did not budge, even when Jessie added her strength to his. They gave up when they saw their efforts were futile. Diego tugged at the padlock again, but it would not open.

"Perhaps I should break the lock and look inside," he suggested. "I'd have the right; the cave is on our land."

"But what if it was your brother who brought it here? Wouldn't he be angry?"

"He would be very angry," Diego agreed. "Perhaps it does belong to Felipe. He and I played in the cave when we were children, and he's the only one I can think of who'd use it."

"Could it belong to Don Antonio?"

Diego shook his head. "No. Putting something like this in here isn't a thing he would do. I don't suppose he even

146

remembers that there's a cave on the ranch, though I'm sure he must have known at one time. It's Felipe's, I'm sure."

"Well, it isn't my affair, of course," Jessie said.

"Of course," Diego agreed. "I'll leave it alone until I can ask him about it."

Jessie nodded and started toward her horse. After a moment, Diego followed her.

"Day after tomorrow?" he said, the note of pleading in his voice more urgent than before. "Promise me, Jessie!"

Jessie kissed him lightly before replying. "I'll try. But don't come here unless I send word. If you do, you'll only be disappointed. Now, you must go, Diego. Teresa and Ki should be getting here very soon."

"There's only one trail they can take," he said. "Ride with me to the place where it forks, Jessie. Even if it's only two miles to the fork, we'll be together that much longer."

Seeing no real reason to refuse him, Jessie nodded. "All right. But promise me that when we get to the fork you'll ride on home without any argument."

"I give you my word," Diego replied.

Carrying with them the sweet-sad memories of passion spent, they talked but little as they rode along the bluff until it tapered off in the general downslope of the terrain. A half mile beyond, they reached the fork in the trail.

"Day after tomorrow?" Diego asked.

"I've told you, if I can. And remember your promise, Diego. Ride on home now. I'll wait here for Teresa and Ki."

"My word is good."

Toeing his horse ahead, he rode off on the trail to Rancho Almagre. Jessie watched Diego's back until he disappeared into the trees, then dismounted and led her mount a little way off the trail to a small stand of head-high seedling pines that stood at the edge of the matured forest. When she walked into the grove, Jessie found the shaded ground under the small trees was thick with pine needles and warm from a full day of sunshine.

Looking at the sun, she saw that its bottom rim still had a way to drop before touching the horizon. Belatedly, she realized that a combination of circumstances—the time spent in the semidarkness of the cave, the unfamiliar terrain with its jagged horizon line so different from that of the flat Texas prairie—had distorted her time sense.

With the realization, Jessie changed her plan to ride down the trail to meet Ki and Teresa. After looping the reins loosely around a low-hanging branch, she sat down at the base of the tree and leaned back against its rough bark. After a few moments, the warmth of the pine needles and the quiet peace of the late-afternoon air began to have their effect. Jessie dozed.

Voices breaking the still air brought Jessie awake. They were still distant from the grove, and she heard them as an undertone of sound rather than recognizable speech. She wondered how long she'd slept, but was sure her nap must have been brief. The sky was still bright and sunlight still dappled the ground where the foliage of the immature pines was thin. Her horse stood quietly where she'd left it, though she saw that the gelding's ears had pricked up and were twitching.

Scrambling to her feet, Jessie walked to the edge of the grove and looked down the trail that led to Big Piney. She saw no one, though the voices were growing steadily louder. Peering down the narrow winding path that disappeared down the slope, she saw flickers of motion between the big boles of the mature trees, but she was unable to see anything clearly.

Jessie walked back to her horse, freed its reins from the

tree, and led it down the trail. The voices were louder now and Jessie frowned. They were not the familiar voices of Teresa and Ki, but of two men talking loudly, angrily. Then the approaching riders emerged from the thick pine grove. One of the riders was a stranger, but even at that distance she recognized the other. He was Diego's twin brother, Felipe.

Recalling Felipe's outburst when she and Ki had encountered him on their way to the Rancho Velarde, Jessie decided instantly that she did not want a second meeting. She turned to lead her horse into the concealment of the trees. One of the approaching animals sensed the presence of the strange horse and neighed. Jessie's gelding answered, starting to rear and toss its head.

Accustomed to riding Sun, her own well-schooled palomino, Jessie had been holding the reins loosely. The gelding's tossing head pulled the leathers from her hands and the animal bolted. It started down the slope toward the approaching riders. Jessie saw that she had no chance to catch the horse. She turned and began running down the slope through the saplings, hoping to find a place to hide in the grove of big pines.

Jessie heard Creighton and Felipe shout at the same time. When she looked back, she saw that they had seen her and had turned their horses in her direction. Doggedly, she continued the unequal race, but even her superbly conditioned muscles were no match for the horses. Her pursuers boxed her between their mounts and Creighton slid out of the saddle to grab her.

"Well, I never figured I'd get this close to the high-and-mighty Miss Jessie Starbuck!" he gloated. "Go catch her horse, Felipe! We'll just take her along with us to our camp!"

Chapter 14

Ahead of Ki and Teresa the trail through the forest of big pines twisted like a writhing serpent.

"I'll be glad when we get out of these trees and off this winding trail," Teresa said.

"We'll be at the fork in just a few more minutes," Ki told her. "And from there on to the ranch the trail is easier."

"Yes, but it's going to be dark before we get back to the hacienda, and Grandfather always worries about me if I'm not in the house by sundown."

"I was just thinking that Jessie must be wondering why we haven't shown up by now," Ki told her. "But I'm sure she'll understand why we're late better than Don Esteban will."

Teresa sighed. "I envy the relationship you and Jessie have, Ki, even if I don't quite understand it."

"There's nothing to understand," Ki said. "Alex Starbuck gave me a place in the world when I needed one. When he was killed, I saw that Jessie would need me to help her and offered to serve her just as I'd served Alex. It was not long before we became friends, in the same way that her father and I were."

"That's what she's told me, but I didn't really believe her until she suggested telling you she was going to meet—" Teresa stopped short as they came in sight of the cave. "That's funny," she went on. "Jessie's not here. At least, if she is, I don't see her."

Ki dismounted and entered the mouth of the cave. In a moment he returned shrugging. "She's not inside, either," he said.

Teresa frowned. "Ki, I don't understand why—"

"Perhaps I'm beginning to," Ki broke in. "I knew there was something bothering me about this trail, Teresa. Look at it. When we went over it earlier on the way to Big Piney, there were only a few hoofprints on it. Now, the ground's all torn up."

Teresa leaned forward in her saddle to see the hoofprints more clearly. "Yes," she said. "Now that we're past the stretch used by the loggers, there shouldn't be this many horses passing along here. These trails are only used a lot when the *vaqueros* take the cattle to the high range in spring and bring them back in the fall."

"We're not far from the place where the trail to the cave forks off," Ki said with a frown. "Let's see what it looks like. The only prints on it should be the ones left by Diego's horse."

When they reached the fork, Ki pointed to the pocked earth. He said soberly, "Whoever rode this way turned off here on this small trail. Eight or ten riders, perhaps more. And I don't suppose I need to tell you what that means."

"No. I can read the tracks as well as you can, Ki. Remember, I grew up in this Rio Arriba country."

"Tell me what you read in the tracks, then," Ki suggested. "Let's see if we agree."

151

"It's very plain," Teresa said. "The men who attacked Big Piney came back this way. And they must have seen Jessie and taken her with them."

"Not without a fight. And Jessie's a good shot."

"She was unarmed, Ki," Teresa confessed. "She left her pistol at the hacienda; she didn't want to wear it because she was going to meet Diego."

Ki frowned. "I didn't notice that she wasn't wearing her gunbelt!"

"Perhaps because she knew you wouldn't approve, she wore a sash I gave her. That's why you didn't see."

Ki did not reply. He knew Jessie well enough to understand her need to appear very feminine at times. He said, "I don't like this a bit, Teresa. Jessie couldn't have gone any other direction, either by accident or on purpose. Doesn't this trail also end at the cave?"

"No. It goes up to one of the Rancho Almagre's high-country camps. The Hinojosa's summer cattle range is up in the mountains, just as ours is."

"Then Don Antonio must know that the gang is using it," Ki said, talking to himself as much as to Teresa. "And perhaps he was even responsible for Diego luring Jessie here today, to give that gang a chance—"

"No!" Teresa broke in. "Don Antonio knows about the gang, I suppose, but Diego wouldn't have anything to do with a scheme like that, Ki. Believe me! Felipe, yes. He's mean and hateful. But not Diego."

"I'll soon find out," Ki told her. Then, his tone growing even more serious than it had been, he went on, "You know I've got to follow these hoofprints, Teresa. You don't mind going on to your hacienda alone, do you? If you hurry, you'll get there before dark."

"I'd rather go with you, Ki. Maybe I can help."

"No," Ki said, shaking his head. "I couldn't face either

Jessie or Don Esteban if I allowed you to go and something happened to you. Surely you can understand that."

For a moment Teresa was silent; then she nodded. "Yes, I suppose I do. But I've got a better idea than going home. I'll ride back to Big Piney, Ki. It's closer than our hacienda, and I can alert the men there. If they head out right away, they'll catch up with you soon."

Ki thought for a moment, then nodded. "Your idea's better than mine. Go on, Teresa. And get them to hurry."

Ki watched Teresa ride off, then turned his horse up the mountain trail and started for the high country.

Darkness was settling in over the valleys that stretched out below the high ground where Creighton and his men reined in. Jessie looked around and realized that the sprawling mountain meadow where they'd stopped was a summer camp for the Rancho Almagre. The meadow was little more than a quarter mile across, and it lay in a shallow, oval-shaped hollow that was little more than a dimple in the rugged terrain that surrounded it.

A small pole corral, large enough to hold eight or ten horses, stood at one edge of the meadow. A dozen yards from the corral there was an adobe hut, its door sagging and its single window without a pane. A canvas fly had been stretched between four corner poles, covering the area outside the little hut; between it and the hut, soot-blackened stones encircled a fire pit.

Around Jessie, the ragtag group of men that had staged the attack on Big Piney were dismounting. Creighton and Felipe were standing a few feet away from her, watching their defeated, dispirited minions.

Jessie had already taken stock of Felipe Hinojosa, and she devoted her full attention to Creighton. The man she suspected of being a cartel operative was short legged and stocky and running to fat. He had the florid face of a heavy drinker and the gross double chin of a man who ate to excess as well. He wore a low-crowned gray derby hat and a tweed suit, more appropriate for a city than for the still-untamed Rio Arriba country.

Creighton turned to look at Jessie and read the distaste that showed on her face. He came over to stand beside her horse, and Felipe followed him.

"This place ain't fancy, but it's just a start," Creighton told Jessie. "Felipe and me have got a lot of things to do here. Give us a summer, and you'll see a lot of changes."

"Hold your tongue, Creighton!" Felipe snapped. "From what you've told me, this Starbuck woman and her father before her have prevented you and your friends from carrying out a number of your plans!"

"Oh, hell, Felipe, you don't have to bother about her any longer," Creighton said. "We got her now, and she's as good as finished. Soon as I get word to my boss in Denver, he's going to tell me to get rid of her. The way I see it, he can't do much else."

"You would be wise to talk less and do more," Felipe retorted. "Weeks will pass before you can get your orders about her. In the meantime, the Anglos at the sawmill must be dealt with, or they will continue to delay our plans."

"That ain't all my fault," Creighton replied. "You was going to give me twice as many men as you've come up with so far to do the job I come here for. With two of 'em shot in that fool fracas at Big Piney today, we only got six left. Like I told you from the start, ten's the least I need to handle them damn loggers."

"You had eight," Felipe said. "And you and I made ten."

"Sure. But them damn fools didn't take orders! They begun shooting before you and me got up where we could do any good."

"And is that my fault?" Felipe demanded hotly.

"Maybe so, maybe not. All I'm telling you is, I got to have ten men. From the way you bragged when we made our deal in Santa Fe, I figured this part of the territory'd have a lot more guns for hire than you been able to scrape up."

Jessie now began to see the full extent of the plan in which Creighton had obviously enlisted Felipe's aid. From her own battles with the cartel, and from the many notes Alex had left detailing his investigation of its operations, Jessie had grown wise in understanding the cartel's ways. She was now sure of much more than just what the conversation between Creighton and Diego had revealed.

The words of the two men only confirmed the suspicion she'd mentioned to Ki after the settlers at Big Piney had confided their problems to her. She needed no more proof to convince her that Creighton was one of the cartel's field operatives and that he had been sent to bring the timber resources of the Rio Arriba under the control of the sinister group of European financiers and industrialists.

"I have done the best I can to find the men you have," Felipe snapped. "It is you who've given them their orders! You are to blame for today's failure, not me!"

"Hell, today was a good one, Felipe!" Creighton retorted. "We got the Starbuck dame! She's worth a dozen Big Pineys!"

"To you, perhaps," Felipe snarled. "Not to me! When do you intend to finish your job here, and turn command of the Rio Arriba over to me as you promised?"

"Now, you know that ain't going to happen soon," Creighton replied. "We agreed you wouldn't take over until old Don Antonio dies—and that ain't going to be long, from the little I seen of him. But what about that brother of yours?"

"Diego will die soon after my father does. I will see to that myself," Felipe replied, his voice coolly casual.

"Fair enough." Creighton nodded. "But remember, I got to be sure you can do the job before I give you free rein up here. My boss in Denver's got big plans for this place, like I told you. He's going to make the Rio Arriba the main headquarters for everything from the Mississippi clear out to the Pacific Ocean."

Jessie's eyes opened wide when she heard Creighton's boast. She understood its full implications in an instant. She'd seen enough of the isolated high country of northern New Mexico Territory to realize that it would provide the cartel with an operating center that would require an army to uproot.

Now, Jessie resolved that the plan must be smashed before even the first step toward cartel control could be taken. With her mind on the conversation between Creighton and Felipe rather than on her own predicament, she stirred restlessly in the saddle. Her movement attracted their attention.

"What do you propose to do with her?" Felipe asked, indicating Jessie with a disdainful flick of his hand.

"Why, she's going to stay right here," Creighton said. "She's a right pretty woman, and after I get through with her, I bet the men would be able to keep her busy for quite some time."

Though Jessie's blood ran cold when she heard Creighton's words, she showed no outward sign of her dismay. She stared into the distance, ignoring him and Felipe.

"You'd turn her over to them?" Felipe frowned.

"Why, sure," Creighton replied. His voice held no more feeling than if he'd been discussing trading a horse or butchering a steer. He went on, "I know my boss is going to tell me to get rid of her, and she'd sure keep the men settled down in this godforsaken place while we get a few more gunslingers to clean up them loggers and wait for fresh orders from Denver."

"I suppose you're right," Felipe agreed. His tone was as coldly callous as Creighton's had been. "Don Esteban Velarde would not like what you propose, but he would not dare to invade Hinojosa land, even if he knew she was here."

"It's settled, then," Creighton said. "You bring me about six more men, and we'll wipe out them loggers. Then we can go ahead with the plans you and me have talked about."

Creighton turned to look at the ruffians who were straggling back from the corral after unsaddling their horses, and he motioned for two of them to come up. When they were within easy earshot, he told them, "Take the woman to the shack. And pass the word to your friends that she'll be yours in a day or so, soon as I've had my fill of her."

Ki pushed his horse along the winding trail, following the hoofprints of the gang's horses. Dusk was settling slowly, the lingering twilight of high altitudes giving way to darkening sky. By now, he was certain that Jessie had been captured by the outlaw band retreating from its raid on Big Piney. He watched the sky anxiously. He did not know how far he had to go, but he wanted to reach the end of his quest with enough light left for him to survey the ground.

In the fast-fading twilight, Ki saw a sudden puff of smoke rising ahead, a wide dark ribbon against a sky that was almost as dark. A veteran of many camps, he recognized at once what the smoke meant. It was the sign of a newly lighted fire. He reined in and tethered his horse beside the trail where it would serve as a signal to the Big Piney men who would be arriving soon. Then he started on foot toward the diminishing column of smoke.

A rise lay just ahead. Looking at the abrupt line of its crest silhouetted against the sky, Ki was sure that beyond it he would encounter a hollow; all the signs told him he was on the lip of a long-extinct volcano. He could see no lookout anywhere along the crest, and he used special caution as he ascended.

When Ki reached the rim, he dropped to his belly and crawled forward for the last few yards. As he'd expected, he was looking down into a shallow volcanic crater. The adobe shack drew Ki's attention first, but only briefly. He looked near the fire to see if Jessie was visible in its light, but she was not. The flames illuminated the area under the canvas fly, but he did not see her there, either.

Pushing aside his frustration, Ki counted the number of men wandering aimlessly around the blaze, but his count of seven told him too little. He knew he'd accounted for two of the Big Piney raiders, but the tracks he'd followed had been so overlaid and confused that he'd been unable to tell how many had returned to the hideout. Since he'd never seen Creighton, he had no way of knowing for sure whether he was one of the seven men he'd tallied.

Ki turned his attention to the other features of the hollow. He could see the poles of the corral, but it was at such a distance from the fire that he could not count the number of horses it contained. There was nothing further in the valley to examine, so he returned his attention to the adobe hut.

Even though he could not see into the dilapidated little structure, Ki was positive that Jessie must be inside. There was no other place she could be. He tried to squint through the window, but he could see no movement. Still, he was sure that Jessie must be in the adobe hut, probably tied up, as there was no guard outside the door.

Ki saw no reason to delay his effort to rescue Jessie. He stood up, stepped over the rim of the crater, and started walking toward the hut.

Chapter 15

After being half-carried, half-dragged into the adobe hut by Creighton's hired killers, all that Jessie could do was to lie motionless for several minutes. The interior of the shack was dark, and she did not stir until her captors kindled their cooking fire between the canvas fly and the hut. Then she began taking stock of her situation. In the flickering half-light that crept into the adobe, she could see now that her ankles had been bound with a rawhide pigging string; exploring her wrist bonds with her fingertips told her that another of the long thin thongs had been used to secure her arms behind her back.

As the fire outside grew brighter and a bit more light came in through the open door and glassless window, she saw that the hut contained only a rumpled heap of blankets along one wall, and a chair and a small oblong table near the window.

When she saw nothing that offered any help in her present situation, Jessie put all her attention to trying to make sense of the intermittent snatches of talk she heard from the men around the fire. She strained her ears, but was able to make out only an occasional word or phrase. Soon the smell of meat cooking floated into the hut on the light night breeze, telling Jessie that the men who'd captured her were cooking their supper.

Realizing that she was not likely to be disturbed for some time, Jessie relaxed as much as her bonds would permit. She wriggled across the dirt floor to a corner, raised her shoulders, and, bracing them against the wall while she pushed with her feet, worked herself into a sitting position. The change did not really improve her situation, but it made her feel less helpless.

She began working on her bonds, straining to move her arms up and down as much as she could in the hope of working some slack in the cruel thongs. She had no way of knowing how long she'd been at her fruitless efforts, but after what seemed a very long time she heard footsteps thudding on the hard earth. She stopped straining, and was sitting motionless when Creighton came through the door.

"I guess you ain't used to sitting on the floor where you come from, but that's the best you'll find here," he said.

Jessie did not reply, but gazed at him steadily.

"Cat's got your tongue, I see," Creighton went on. "Well, you ain't going to be here long. From all I heard about the trouble you've given the outfit I work for, they'll tell me to get rid of you soon as I let 'em know I got you."

Jessie could not halt the involuntary lifting of her eyebrows when she heard Creighton's threat. He was not cut to the pattern of the typical cartel operative. Those she'd encountered in the past had never revealed their connection with the sinister international group; in fact, none of them had even spoken except when necessary. She still remained silent, and her refusal to speak angered her captor.

"I'll make you open that mouth of yours before I'm

finished with you, Miss High-and-Mighty Starbuck!" he grated. "And when I get through with you and hand you over to my men, you'll be yelling your damned swelled-up head off! Now just lay there and think about what you got coming until I get back!"

After Creighton stomped angrily out of the cabin, Jessie sat quietly for a few moments. Creighton's open admission that he was working for the cartel both bothered and puzzled her. She could not decide whether he was as ignorant of the group's code of silence as he seemed to be, or whether he'd been acting out a cleverly conceived plan designed to snare her into talking as freely as she had.

Then she realized that, whatever Creighton's objectives, he had the power to carry them out. She dismissed her conjectures and went back to work trying to free her hands.

"There is still no sign of them, Bartolome?" Don Esteban asked when the *mayordomo* came into the parlor carrying a tray bearing the old man's predinner glass of sherry.

"Not yet, *patrón*," Bartolome replied. "A moment ago, I went to look from the top-floor window, but the trail is bare."

"It isn't like Teresa to be late," Don Esteban said, frowning.

"Do not worry yourself, *patrón*," Bartolome said. "It is not yet fully dark. They will be here soon."

"Delay dinner until they arrive, Bartolome. I will have no appetite until I know they are safe. And bring me the sherry decanter. I think I will need more than a single glass this evening."

Don Esteban sat sipping his sherry until Bartolome returned with the decanter, and by then he had reached a decision. He said, "Tell Benavides, Peralta, and Morales to have their horses saddled and ready in a half hour. And see

162

to getting my light carriage harnessed."

"May I offer an opinion, *patrón?*" the *mayordomo* asked.

"Of course."

"A *carreta* would be a better choice than the carriage. The trail to the pine woods is very rough in places."

Don Esteban nodded. "A *carreta*, then. And one thing more. The *indio*, Carlos—he still lives in the *placita?*"

"Yes, *patrón.*"

"Tell him to be ready to ride with us. He is the best tracker we have. And Bartolome, rifles for myself and you."

"Understood, *patrón.*" Bartolome nodded. "I will bring lanterns, too; he'll need them to see the tracks."

"Bring what you please," Don Esteban said impatiently. "We have no time to waste! We must start at once!"

"Do not concern yourself too greatly, *patrón,*" the *mayordomo* urged. "Teresa and our guests will surely be back before the half hour has passed."

"I will be pleased if they are," the old *hacendado* said. "But even after three hundred years, the Rio Arriba is still a wild and violent land. I do not propose to risk the life of my only heir. Now go, Bartolome."

As Ki started down into the little saucer-shaped valley, he made no effort to hide. His training had taught him that men who have been looking into a source of light, even one as small as the cooking fire that burned near the tent fly, cannot see when they stare into darkness.

Though he was careful to move silently, Ki walked quickly until he was within a dozen yards of the camp. Then he dropped flat and began crawling toward the adobe hut. He might have been another of the wavering, formless shadows cast by the men who stood around the fire pit or hunkered down beside it while they watched the food they were cooking.

163

Ki had almost reached the shack when he saw Creighton start walking toward it. Ki risked moving faster than he knew was safe to cover the short distance that remained. Keeping the hut between Creighton and his own moving figure, he reached the hut and rolled into the deep shadow that veiled the wall away from the fire just as the cartel operative went inside.

As he strained his ears to hear the conversation between Jessie and her captor, Ki's reaction to Creighton's open admission of his cartel connection was much the same as hers. He paid no attention to the threats, secure in the knowledge that he would free Jessie within seconds after she'd been left in the shack alone. He gave Creighton time to return to the fire before snaking silently around the corner of the hut to the window. With a single fluid move he levered himself through the opening.

"I was wondering when you'd get here," Jessie said calmly. "But where did you leave Teresa?"

"She went back to Big Piney for help," Ki told her. "I didn't want to lose any time before following Creighton's gang."

Ki had slipped his *tanto* knife from its sheath and was severing Jessie's bonds with its razor-keen edge. Jessie began rubbing her wrists, which bore creases from the thongs.

"And you didn't have any trouble picking up the trail?"

"No," he replied without interrupting his task. "I've been outside under the window for the past few minutes, listening to you and Creighton talking. You know, I wonder about this man Creighton. Does he seem to you to be very careless and talkative for a cartel operative?"

"I've been wondering the same thing, Ki." Jessie began rubbing her ankles as the thong fell away under Ki's careful slicing. "If he is, they must be scraping the bottom of the barrel. But he must be, or he wouldn't have known about

164

the way we've been fighting them."

"Perhaps we'll find out later," Ki said as he straightened up and sheathed the thin curved blade. "Can you walk, or are your feet too numb?"

"I might need a little help, but I'll manage," she told him, flexing her knees experimentally.

Ki helped Jessie to her feet. She swayed for a moment, and stumbled when she tried a tentative step, but she stayed erect. Dropping to his knees, Ki began kneading the calves of Jessie's legs to restore life to their cramped muscles. With both hands busy at the task he'd taken on, he was slower than usual in reaching for a *shuriken* when footsteps grated on the hard ground outside, growing steadily louder as they approached the door.

Jessie reacted at once by dropping to the dirt floor and rolling to the wall that was in the deepest shadow. Ki's hand had just reached the pocket of his leather vest when one of the gunmen came in carrying a tin plate filled with food. The man dropped the plate when he saw Ki, and his hand swept to his cross-draw holster.

Ki had his fingers on a *shuriken*, but he was not yet holding it in a throwing grip when the man in the doorway swung the revolver toward him. In the instant required for Ki to adjust his fingers on the star-shaped blade, the gunman triggered off a shot. As Ki's *shuriken* spun to the man's throat, the slug from the pistol tore into the calf of Ki's leg.

As the gunman's revolver sagged, he loosed a second shot that sent a bullet into the dust between Ki and the door. The other men, sitting around the fire, were dropping their plates and running toward the shack when Ki glanced past the crumpling figure of the man who'd wounded him.

Ignoring his wound, Ki slid out another throwing blade and sent it whirling into the face of the next man who showed in the open doorway. Ki managed to get to his feet while he was taking out a third *shuriken*, and he was ready with it when another of the outlaws blocked the light coming through the open window.

Hampered by his wound, throwing at an awkward angle, Ki loosed the *shuriken* and saw it cut into the attacker's chest. With the star-pointed blade slicing into his body, the gunman turned and staggered away from the window.

Jessie saw the first gunman's pistol lying on the floor just inside the door. She rolled across the floor and reached for the gun, closing her hand around its grip in time to raise the weapon and fire at the next attacker who silhouetted himself against the firelight's glow. The man who'd been her target spun around, his move taking him out of the range of Jessie's vision.

From the fire, Creighton's voice rose in a shout. "Get back, you damn fools! She's got Stub's gun! Keep outa the line of fire from that door!"

From the area in front of the hut, running footsteps scraped on the soil as the attackers hurried to obey. Then a hoarse voice called, "Keep outa the way of the window, too! I got some kinda knife in my gut when I tried to shoot through it!"

Inside the cabin, Jessie had stretched prone, peering through the doorway in search of another target. In the rectangle to which her vision was limited, she failed to find one. Ki was limping to the window. He stood at one side of the opening and angled his head to look outside.

"I can see two of them, but they're out of throwing range," he told Jessie.

"There's nobody in sight from here," she replied. "And if this gun's loaded the way most gunfighters do, I've only got two shots left."

Ki left the window and hobbled over to join her, and Jessie saw for the first time that he'd been hit. She exclaimed, "You're wounded, Ki! How badly?"

"I haven't had time to look yet." Ki pulled up the leg of his loose trousers. Blood was trickling from a raw crease a hand's span above his ankle. He glanced at the wound and said, "It's not really bad, but I'm afraid the slug grazed my Achilles tendon." He tried an experimental step, but his foot buckled and only his superb muscular control kept him from falling. "That's it, all right," he went on. "I don't have any feeling in my foot."

"Let me put a bandage on it, Ki. I've got a bandanna."

"It's not bleeding that much, Jessie. But for a while, I won't be able to use my leg. I'll probably get the use of it back in a few hours, but right now—"

Jessie broke in, "Right now, it looks like we'll have to stay here and fight instead of getting away."

"We don't have much to fight with, Jessie. I've only got four *shuriken* and my *tanto*."

"And unless I'm wrong . . ." Jessie thumbed the revolver's hammer to half cock and spun the cylinder. "I wasn't. Two more shells left."

"And how many men are out there now? I counted seven when I was watching from the rim of the valley."

"There were eight all together," Jessie replied, "including Creighton and Felipe."

"Yes." Ki nodded. "I saw Felipe. It's obvious that he's working with the cartel."

"Yes. We'll have to find out how he got hooked up with Creighton. Before they put me in this place, I heard Creighton mention something about having met Felipe in Santa Fe, but I don't know any of the details."

"That's not important now," Ki said quickly. "We'd better decide how to handle things. The man in the doorway's dead, and two others are wounded, but we don't know how badly. We have two shells and four *shuriken* and we have

167

to deal with—how many, Jessie? Five? Six? Seven?"

"At least five. I'd say our best bet is to stay right where we are. Even a rifle slug won't go through these adobe walls."

"Then you take the window and I'll take the door," Ki said. "And we'd better get set now, because they'll start moving in on us within the next few minutes."

"Am I mistaken, Bartolome, or did I see a light ahead?" Don Esteban asked, raising his voice to make himself heard over the creaking of the *caretta*'s high wooden wheels.

"I think you are not, *patrón*. I was sure I saw it gleaming myself before we started down this incline."

"Then the light was real," the old *hidalgo* muttered, more to himself than to the steward.

"*Sí, patrón,*" Bartolome said. "And it was on the trail to Rancho Almagre."

"What mischief would bring the Hinojosas out at night?" Don Esteban frowned. "Unless Teresa and her friends—"

"Don't disturb yourself, Don Esteban," the steward urged. "Mischief and evil travel in the dark, not with lights. And we will find out soon what they mean."

Don Esteban was seated in a sturdy high-backed chair that the steward had lashed to the bed of the *carreta*. Bartolome stood in the front of the low-slung cart, handling the reins. Carlos, the wizened tracker, sat on the floor behind the chair, and the three men of the escort rode ahead of the vehicle. Bartolome had fastened lanterns to the front poles that supported the high slatted sides of the cart.

"I suppose you are right," the old *hidalgo* muttered.

He settled back in the chair, his eyes searching the blackness ahead as the party moved slowly forward on the rutted trail. The *carreta* reached the bottom of the slope and creaked up the next rise. Ahead, what had been only a glint of

168

brightness could now be seen as a pair of carriage lights. Silhouetted against their nimbus, the black forms of several mounted men were visible as well.

"It is someone coming from the Rancho Almagre, Bartolome," Don Esteban said. "Could it be that Teresa and her friends have met with trouble there?"

"Let us hope not," Bartolome answered. "But wait, *patrón*, we will know in a moment or two."

"I cannot wait!" Don Esteban snapped. He raised his voice and called to the escort, "Morales! Ride ahead and find out who is in the carriage!" Even as Don Esteban was speaking, he saw that one of the horsemen who'd been riding in advance of the carriage was spurring toward the *carreta*. "Wait, Morales. We will know soon enough." When the rider came into the circle of light cast by the lanterns, Don Esteban recognized him at once. "Diego Hinojosa!" he exclaimed.

"*A sus órdenes*, Don Esteban," the young man replied. He swung out of the saddle and started toward the *carreta*. As he walked, he went on, "You will be happy to know that Teresa is in the carriage with Don Antonio."

"Teresa? Is she—"

"Be calm, Don Esteban," Diego said. He climbed into the *carreta*. "Teresa has suffered no harm. But there are others with us—"

"Of course," Don Esteban broke in. "Her guest, Miss Starbuck, and her companion, Ki."

Diego hesitated for a moment, then told the old man, "I'm afraid not, Don Esteban. They are some men from the Big Piney settlement."

"But surely Teresa—"

Diego interrupted to say, "Perhaps you should let Teresa tell you herself what has happened. The carriage is almost here. She will explain everything."

Almost before Diego had finished speaking, the carriage had come to a halt a few yards ahead of the party from the Rancho Velarde. Teresa ran up to the *carreta,* and Bartolome helped her climb into it. She went to Don Esteban's chair and dropped to her knees beside it.

"What is this about, Teresa?" he demanded. "Why did not you and your guests return as you had planned?"

"There is a good reason, Grandfather," Teresa said. "We found outlaws attacking the loggers at Big Piney. Ki went to help the villagers, and soon the outlaws were driven off, but to escape danger from them as they ran, Jessie and I were separated. They captured Jessie, and Ki followed them to try to help her."

"And you do not know where they are?" Don Esteban asked.

"I haven't finished, Grandfather," Teresa replied. "Ki insisted on leaving at once, while I waited for some of the men from Big Piney. They are with us now."

"How is it that you are with the Hinojosas?" Don Esteban asked her. "Why did you not come home when you needed help?"

Diego broke in, "One of our herders was near the logging village, Don Esteban. He came to inform us of the shooting he had heard. Don Antonio and I started to investigate the shooting, and we met Teresa and the loggers on the trail."

"We were following the outlaws, you see," Teresa said quickly. "We knew Jessie and Ki would need help."

Don Esteban shook his head. "It is all very confusing," he said. "This fighting and chasing and following. But why did you not come home to me for help, Teresa?"

"Because Don Antonio thinks he knows where the outlaws have been hiding," she replied. "He will tell you more, Grandfather. We're wasting time talking, when we should be following Jessie and Ki!"

"You are right." The old *hidalgo* nodded. "And now that we have met, I must go with you. Miss Starbuck and Ki are our guests!" He turned to Diego. "Where is this place, Diego?"

"One of our summer camps in a hollow of the *tierra alta,*" the young man said. "The trail forks off this one."

"I know the place you speak of," Don Esteban said. "It is on the land Don Antonio—"

Teresa broke in quickly. "Talking can wait, Grandfather! We must hurry now! Jessie and Ki may need our help!"

"Yes, certainly!" Don Esteban agreed. "Tell Don Antonio we are joining you. And since I know the trail there as well as he does, we will lead the way!"

★

Chapter 16

Ki's prediction of how long they would have before Creighton's men attacked proved faulty. He and Jessie peered through the window, watching the area lighted by the fire. Nothing happened, though. The gang milled around Creighton and Felipe, but paid no attention to the adobe shack.

"I don't think they know how little ammunition we have," Ki suggested as the minutes passed.

"Either that, or Creighton just can't persuade them to do anything," Jessie replied. "From what I overheard, they're not regular cartel killers, just hired gunmen that Felipe's managed to scrape up for him."

"We could still make a run for it," Ki suggested.

"We wouldn't last long," she said. "We'd be on foot, and they have horses. With that wounded leg, you couldn't move fast enough or far enough for us to have a chance. Let's rest as much as we can now. We'll need all our strength when they attack us."

Jessie leaned against the wall and closed her eyes. After a few minutes she dozed, waking only when Ki pressed her arm.

"It looks like they're getting ready to move," he said.

Jessie joined him in looking out the window again. The gang was scattering, fanning out from the point where the men had been standing during their long discussion. At some time while Jessie slept the fire had been replenished, dispelling the gloom.

"I'd give a lot to have a full moon tonight," Jessie said as the last of Creighton's men disappeared in the darkness. "What do you think they're going to do now?"

"There's not much they can do except start shooting again," Ki replied. "They'll probably form a half circle, to increase their chances of hitting us."

"But they can't see to aim in the dark!" Jessie objected. "As long as we keep below the window sill, they don't have much chance of hitting us. They'll still be shooting blind!"

"Of course. I'd guess Creighton's getting edgy, though. And they're pretty sure to have plenty of ammunition."

"Well, they know we can't do much shooting back," Jessie said. "It's lucky we're in this little shack instead of a tent."

"Yes, we'll be all right as long as we don't get in the line of fire from slugs coming through the door or window," Ki agreed. "And adobe won't burn, so we don't have to worry about them setting the shack on fire."

A rifle cracking in the darkness beyond range of the firelight gave Jessie and Ki the answers to their questions. The first shot was followed by a ragged volley. Slugs thunked into the adobe walls, and two of the bullets whizzed in through the window, but Jessie and Ki were flattened out on the dirt floor by then. The bullets did no damage except to add to the pocks already in the walls opposite.

"Have you been counting the blasts, Ki?" Jessie asked. "I have, and there are only five rifles being fired."

"That's what I counted, too. So we put three of them out

173

of commission. And their second shots didn't come from the same places the first did, so they're moving after every shot, even if they know we've only got a couple of rounds in that pistol."

More shots rang out. As the echoes of the firing died, Jessie said, "The wind must've changed, Ki. I can smell the smoke from the fire now, and I couldn't a few minutes ago."

"Smoke, of course!" Ki exclaimed. "Not fire!"

Almost before Ki had finished speaking, a wad of burning cloth sailed through the door, followed by a second and then a third. There was no letup in the rifle fire, slugs kept hitting the adobe walls. The wads burned slowly, the flames blue in the darkness of the shack, filling it with acrid smoke. Jessie and Ki began coughing and their eyes started to water.

"Keep your head close to the floor, Jessie," Ki said as he started crawling to the nearest flame.

He slid his *tanto* from its sheath as he moved. When he could reach the burning bundle, he thrust the curved blade into it and flipped it out the door. He rolled to the second wad and pushed the knife into it, but before he could throw it, two more burning bundles sailed through the door into the cabin.

"They can throw them in faster than you can throw them back out!" Jessie gasped. "We've got to get out of here, Ki!"

"Use the window, then!" Ki told her. "And crawl behind the shack as soon as you hit the ground!"

Before Jessie could reach the window, a volley of rifle shots broke the air. These shots were from a greater distance than those of the cartel gang, the firing heavier and more sustained than what they'd heard before.

"Somebody else is out there!" Ki exclaimed.

"It's the loggers, of course!" Jessie said between bouts

of coughing. "Teresa must have brought them here at last!"

"No more burning wads, either," Ki said. He was coughing as badly as she was. "Maybe we can risk leaving, Jessie. If we crawl out the door and keep the shack between us and the rifles, we ought to be able to make it."

"Creighton's gang will be too busy to pay any attention to us," she wheezed. "Come on, Ki! Let's go!"

They wormed across the floor to the door. Ki stuck his head out and gazed into the darkness. No bullets were hitting the shack now, but he could see muzzle flashes spurting from the crater's rim and from the valley floor as shots shattered the night. He reached through the door and groped for Jessie's hand.

"We've got to keep together," he said, "even if we're not going very far. I think the safest place for us is just around the corner of the shack. It's not a perfect shield, but it's the only one we have."

They crawled outside and lay quietly. Within a few minutes the fresh night air had cleared the smoke from their lungs and they were breathing normally again.

Jessie said, "Teresa got the men from Big Piney here without any time to spare, Ki. We were lucky."

"Very. They're wiping out the gang. I only see three rifles firing from down here now."

They watched and listened as the firing continued. Soon there were only two rifles answering the gunfire from the rim, and then there were no more shots from the crater floor.

"I'm sure the Big Piney men will be coming down here now," Ki told Jessie. "When they're close enough, you'd better call to them. They might shoot if they heard a man's voice."

Matches flared on the rim as the lights of Don Antonio's coach and the lanterns on the *carreta* were rekindled. Jessie and Ki watched with growing surprise as the procession of their rescuers wound down to the valley floor.

"Over here!" Jessie called to them as they approached.

In a moment, a babble of excited voices broke the now-still air. Attracting no attention in the hubbub, Diego moved quietly to Jessie's side.

In a half whisper he said, "Tell me truthfully, Jessie. My brother was with those men who brought you here, was he not?"

Jessie hesitated for only a moment before answering. "Yes, he was, Diego."

"Then he will be among the dead." Diego's face grew somber as he went on, "I must ask a favor of you. I do not want Don Antonio to see Felipe's corpse. Can you persuade him and Don Esteban to leave soon? Tell Don Antonio that since this is Hinojosa land, I will stay and do what is necessary."

"I—I can try," Jessie replied. She frowned thoughtfully and added, "I'm sure Don Esteban will start at once if I tell him Teresa and I are very tired. You might have to help persuade Don Antonio to go, though."

"I have an idea," Diego said. "Will you help me try it?"

"Of course."

She walked beside Diego to Don Antonio's carriage. The old grandee was sitting alone, staring into the darkness. Diego opened the carriage door and said, "May I ask you to do a favor for Miss Starbuck?"

"Of course. What is it?"

"She is very tired," Diego replied. "And so is Teresa. It would be a kindness to these ladies if you offered to take them in your carriage to the Rancho Velarde, and save them from being exhausted still more by riding in Don Esteban's *carreta*."

"I will—" Don Antonio stopped short and frowned. "But if they ride, I must also ask Esteban Velarde to share my

176

carriage as well. It is a matter of *pundonor* that I do so!"

"Don't bother, then, Don Antonio," Jessie said quickly. "I'm sure Teresa and I will be all right in the *carreta*."

"After what you and Teresa have suffered today, that would be unthinkable when I have a comfortable carriage!" the old man said. He stopped, sighed, and went on, "Very well, Diego." Turning to Jessie, he said, "Miss Starbuck, if you will be so kind as to ask him, I will take Don Esteban as well."

For the first few moments after the carriage rolled away from the crater, its occupants did not speak. It was clear from the faces of both the old men that they were under a strain, and neither Jessie nor Teresa wanted to speak first.

Don Esteban finally broke the uncomfortable silence. "I am aware of the great kindness you are showing my granddaughter and her guest," he said.

"*De nada.*" Don Antonio shrugged. "It is a small favor. I need no thanks."

Don Esteban's face stiffened and he turned his head aside.

After a moment, Jessie said, "Don Antonio, Don Esteban, maybe I shouldn't intrude on your private affairs, but speaking as a friend of Teresa, surely you gentlemen can find a way to end your old misunderstanding. It saddens both your families."

"Jessie!" Teresa gasped. "Why do you—"

Jessie motioned for her to be quiet, and went on, "You are both much too honorable to lie or to cheat. Surely there's a way to explain what went wrong so many years ago."

Don Esteban said stiffly, "I would like very much to hear Don Antonio explain how a chest filled with gold coins vanished into thin air! Even a Hinojosa cannot do that!"

"Bah!" Don Antonio snorted. "My family has never had such a chest! I know what was in our strong room when my father died! No chest such as you speak of was there!"

"Then where did my son leave it?" Don Esteban demanded. "I know he carried it to the Rancho Almagre! The day remains carved in my memory. It was the day before he and his wife left to go to the dance given by Don Benito Esquival to celebrate his saint's day. It was when Carlos and his wife were coming home that both were killed by the *lleno furioso!* Such things a man does not forget!"

"Aha!" Don Antonio exclaimed. "I knew your son could not have delivered the chest as you say! I can recall that day just as you do. My father and I had already arrived in Taos to attend that very dance! We would not have been home to receive such a chest—had it even been brought to the Rancho Almagre! Only Diego and Felipe were there on that day!"

Suddenly the memory that had been nagging Jessie's mind took shape and became an idea. She said, "Please! Before you say anything more, I'd like to ask Don Esteban a question."

"Ask, of course, Miss Starbuck," Don Esteban said. "But I do not see what question you could have that would bring light to something that happened when you were a child and did not even know that our families existed."

"Will you describe the chest?" Jessie asked.

"To be sure. It was as long as this"—Don Esteban moved his hands apart to indicate the measurement—"as wide as this"—he spread his hands as he spoke—"and stood this high. It was padlocked, but when Carlos delivered the gold he took the key to give to Don Eusebio."

Jessie glanced out the carriage window. The lights on its sides showed the face of the massive granite cliff that held the cave. She said, "Don Antonio, there is the mouth of a cave a short distance ahead. Will you please ask your coachman to stop when we reach it?"

"What foolishness is—" Don Antonio began, but he stopped when he saw the serious look on Jessie's face. He nodded. "Very well. I am sure you have a reason, Miss Starbuck."

Leaning out of the carriage window, Don Antonio gave the command to the coachman. The carriage rumbled on its lurching way for several more minutes before the coachman reined in. Jessie looked out the window and saw the mouth of the cave, a high black triangle in the face of the tall bluff.

"We must go into the cave," she said. "Teresa, bring one of the carriage lights." She turned to Don Antonio. "I would like to take your rifle with us, if I may."

"Of course," he replied with a puzzling frown. "But if you fear danger—"

"There's no danger," Jessie assured him. "I need the gun for another reason."

They made a strangely ill-assorted procession going into the cavern. Jessie led them to the back, where the chest rested.

When he saw it, Don Esteban exclaimed, "But that is the very chest I sent to the Rancho Almagre so many years ago! How did it get here?"

"We may never know that, Don Esteban," Jessie said. She raised the rifle and with one shot blasted the padlock into a tangled ruin of metal shards. Turning to Don Antonio, she said, "If you'll open the chest . . ."

A puzzled scowl on his face, the old man did as she asked. When he removed the broken padlock and lifted the lid, stacks of gold coins gleamed in the lantern light.

"Madre de Dios!" Don Esteban exclaimed. "It is the money I sent to Rancho Almagre so many years ago! What do you say now, Don Antonio Hinojosa?"

For a moment, Don Antonio stared silently at the stacks of gold coins; then he turned to Don Esteban. Frowning, he asked, "You do not know how the money came to be hidden here?"

Jessie spoke quickly. "Why would Don Esteban have kept silent if he'd known? No, Don Antonio. But you might ask Diego if he or Felipe hid it here as a prank."

"Diego? Felipe?" Don Antonio scowled. "A prank?" He shook his head. "I still do not understand, but I will do as you suggest, Miss Starbuck." Then he turned to Don Esteban. "I have wronged your family, Esteban. For this, I apologize. If you can find it in your heart to forgive—"

"I will not hold a grudge, Antonio," Don Esteban replied a bit stiffly. "But the air is chilly in here, and I'm sure Teresa and Miss Starbuck are tired. Let us postpone our discussion until we reach the Rancho Velarde."

Ki always slept lightly, his sixth sense attuned to the smallest sound. The almost inaudible click of his bedroom door being opened brought him erect in bed, one hand reaching for the *tanto* that lay on the chair close by. The pale light of beginning dawn was brightening the window. The door swung open, and when he saw who his visitor was he relaxed.

"You don't object, do you, Ki?" Teresa asked.

"Of course not. I'm surprised, but a pleasant surprise is a good way to start the day."

"All the exciting things that happened last night kept me awake," Teresa said, moving slowly to the bed. "I looked out my window when you and the men returned, and—well, here I am."

She was tugging at the bow of ribbon that held her long white negligee caught up at her throat. The knot gave way, and when Teresa shrugged her shoulders the filmy garment slid to the floor. Ki looked at her with undisguised admiration as she stood there inviting his gaze.

Teresa was fully a woman in spite of her small stature. Her skin glowed ivory in the dim dawnlight, its smoothness only accentuated by the rosy budded tips of her breasts. Her dark eyes above high cheekbones were a perfect complement to the coal-black hair that outlined her oval face, with its thin, aristocratic nose and voluptuously full red lips.

"You're very beautiful," Ki said. He extended his hand and Teresa clasped it between her palms for a moment before placing it in the warm cleft of her full breasts.

"Aren't you going to invite me to your bed?" she asked.

Ki leaned forward and moved his hand from Teresa's breasts to embrace her waist and pull her to the bed. She fell forward, across his chest. Holding her claspéd to him, Ki bent to kiss her. Her tongue darted between his lips, and she pressed her breasts to his muscular chest, pushing him down on the bed. Ki felt her warm, soft hand trail down his side and move to the cove of his growing excitement.

Ki was content to let Teresa set the style of their embrace. He lay back, responding to her questing tongue by twining it with his own, rolling the tips of her breasts between his steel-strong thumbs and fingertips. Teresa's warm hands had not stopped caressing him, and he was now fully ready.

Teresa broke their kiss with a sigh, lifted her head, and looked down into his almond eyes. "You don't mind being below me?" she asked.

Ki shook his head and said, "Whatever pleases you the most."

Wordlessly, Teresa straddled him and guided him to enter her. She brought her hips down slowly, her head thrown back as he slid into her fully. She planted her hands on Ki's shoulders and pushed herself up, moaning softly as she rolled her hips from side to side.

"You fill me beautifully, Ki," she whispered. "And I've been empty for so long!"

Ki raised his head, and his lips found her breasts again. Teresa cried out with small high-pitched sighs as she continued to roll her hips; then her sighs changed to panting gasps as her thighs quivered and she started rocking frantically to and fro, pressing herself down on Ki's hips.

Minute by minute her movements became jerkier and more spasmodic. Ki grasped her softly rounded buttocks and pulled her to him, moving deeper into her than before, while Teresa bent to seek his lips again as she went into a shaking, writhing spasm. Her entire body quivering, she threw back her head, and small quavering cries burst from her lips until her body suddenly went limp and she fell forward on him with a long, moaning sigh.

Ki lay quietly while Teresa recovered; his only movement was to stroke her smooth back while her quivers faded and she lay quietly again. She raised her head and looked down at him.

"But you're still not finished, Ki," she said. "You fill me just as fully as you did when we first started."

"We haven't really started yet," Ki said, smiling. "Be patient, Teresa. The morning's only beginning."

"Prove it to me," she challenged, her sparkling eyes and smiling lips inviting him.

Ki lifted her bodily and reversed their positions without disturbing the firm bond of flesh that held them together. He looked down on Teresa now as he began stroking slowly. Smiling up at him, she clasped her legs around his lean hips and began to turn her torso from side to side as he thrust.

Ki continued his long, firm stroking until Teresa once again began gasping and moaning, and he did not stop even after she shook into another quivering climax. He slackened his pace only briefly, then gradually increased the tempo of his thrusts until he was stroking with a speed that matched Teresa's breathless writhing.

"Hurry, Ki," she urged. She was trembling on the brink of another climax again, her body quivering, her hips beginning to lose their even rhythm as she rocked them to meet his stroking. "But be with me this time, or I'll think I don't please you."

"I will," Ki sighed.

He did not maintain his control now, and his thrusts grew ragged as he drew near his brink. Teresa's moans grew louder, and Ki knew that she was ready as he drove for the last time and held himself pressed against her trembling body while he peaked and sighed and then lay quietly, happily spent.

Minutes ticked by before Teresa stirred and sighed. She opened her eyes and looked at the rosy dawnglow brightening the window's curtains. "I've stayed longer than I should, Ki," she whispered. "I must go now, but there's always tonight and we can be together again then."

She bent to kiss him softly before slipping on her negligee and going out the door. Ki looked at the brightening window for a moment, and then the exertions of the past day and night caught up with him. Turning over, he was soon asleep again.

"I'd have liked to stay with Teresa a little longer, Ki," Jessie said as their horses carried them along the trail toward Santa Fe.

Ahead of them, they could see long-growing piñon trees beginning to mingle with the taller, more stately pines.

"A week gave us enough rest," Ki replied. "And I know you want to go to Denver to find out about those papers you got out of Creighton's saddlebags."

"I certainly do." Jessie looked back at the ragged horizon, tall mountains thrusting into a cloudless sky. She sighed and said, "We have a beautiful country, Ki. Too beautiful to let it be destroyed by a few greedy men like those in the cartel. If I don't do anything else, I'm going to carry on the fight my father started to keep that from happening."

Watch for

LONE STAR AND THE BUFFALO HUNTERS

thirty-fifth novel in the exciting
LONE STAR
series from Jove

coming in July!